A DARTMOOR MURDER

A gripping crime mystery full of twists

(Inspector John Crow Book 8)

ROY LEWIS

Revised edition 2019
Joffe Books, London
www.joffebooks.com

FIRST PUBLISHED AS
"A RELATIVE DISTANCE" IN 1981

This book is a work of fiction. Names, characters, businesses, organisations, places and events are either the product of the author's imagination or are used fictitiously. Any resemblance to actual persons, living or dead, events or locales is entirely coincidental. The spelling used is British English except where fidelity to the author's rendering of accent or dialect supersedes this. The right of Roy Lewis to be identified as author of this work has been asserted by her in accordance with the Copyright, Designs and Patents Act 1988.

We hate typos too but sometimes they slip through.
Please send any errors you find to
corrections@joffebooks.com
We'll get them fixed ASAP. We're very grateful to eagle-eyed readers who take the time to contact us.

©Roy Lewis

Please join our mailing list for free Kindle crime thriller, detective, and mystery books and new releases.
http://www.joffebooks.com/contact/
ISBN: 978-1-78931-103-7

He that is placed at a great distance from an object is a bad judge of the relative space that separates other objects from it.

Charles Caleb Colton : *Lacon*

NOTE TO THE READER

Please note this book is set in the late 1970s in England, a time before mobile phones and DNA testing, and when social attitudes were very different.

CHAPTER 1

Commander Bill Gray tossed the last of his sandwich to the scurrying ducks at the waterside, and glanced about him in the spring sunshine. The warmth of the morning had brought a considerable number of people into St James's Park, to the benefit of the ducks, and Gray himself was glad of the chance to get out of the office for an hour and wander in the park for a sandwich lunch before proceeding to his appointment with Edward Foster, MP. He glanced at his watch, frowning; he guessed that there might be certain problems arising out of that appointment, because politicians were notoriously inept at understanding the nuances of police procedures, and the man he was waiting for was only too sharp at picking out the problems that might spring from decisions taken without reference to those procedures.

He waited by the railings, a burly, handsome man in his mid-forties, his thick, curly hair now lightly frosted at the temples, his nervous hands, like his eyes never still, tapping a trifle impatiently on the guardrails. After a while he lit a pipe, and stood smoking quietly, half leaning, waiting for the arrival of Detective Superintendent John Crow. A punctual man, John Crow; he would arrive just on time.

He did.

He came striding along the path, a tall, ungainly figure with a hatless domed skull shining in the sunlight, and the deep set of his eyes accentuated by the brightness of the light. Gray knew that John Crow was aware of the way people stared at him, and ignored it, but there would be times when Crow would be hurt by it, too. A warm man, and a committed one, to his job and to his friends.

Commander Gray knew that he was not counted among John Crow's friends.

'Good morning, John,' Gray said, as Crow drew near. He smiled disarmingly. 'Thought it would be nicer if we met out here and went together to our appointment.'

'It's a pleasant enough morning,' Crow agreed. He stood waiting as Gray leaned back against the railing, smoking his pipe in an affable, relaxed manner. 'Are we walking from here?'

'It's not far,' Gray said, nodding. 'You . . . er . . . you finished with the Belton enquiry, I gather?'

'I have.' Crow glanced around at the people wandering about the pond, and added, 'But that's a statement rather than a question; you wouldn't have asked me to come here if you hadn't had something new in mind for me, would you?'

'It's true I don't often call upon you—'

'That's right.' They both were aware of the edge that had crept into their relationship over the years: it had begun with the Marlin case, when Gray had wanted Crow to hold back on certain enquiries and he had refused; it had been sharpened when Gray had tried to make him bow to political pressure in the Rutland murder some years later. But though John Crow could not accept the kinds of pressures that Gray brought upon him from time to time, he was realistic enough to appreciate that Gray himself had a job to do, and part of it was to pick his own way through a minefield of politics and diplomacy. 'No, you don't often call on me, and for that I'm grateful.'

'You're still one of our best men, John,' Gray said quietly. 'For a certain kind of job.'

'We all have our peculiar . . . expertise.'

'Ahh . . . what do you know about mining, John?'

Crow stared at him in surprise as the Commander tapped out his pipe, returned it to his pocket, and began to walk away in the direction of Westminster. 'Mining? Next to nothing.'

'And mining in the Southwest?'

'Nothing at all.'

Commander Gray smiled. 'There's been a fair bit in Devon, over the years. So I understand.'

'I'd heard of mining in Cornwall, but—'

'No, Devon too. In fact, I'm told that mining on Dartmoor goes way back. The records date as far along as 1563. And in the nineteenth century there were five separate mines in operation around the Plymouth area.'

Crow matched his longer stride with Bill Gray's, and asked, 'What were they mining for?'

'Tin, copper, lead. And arsenic, I believe. It may be the Victorian poisoners owed their methods to the Devon mining industry. Makes you think, doesn't it?'

'I'd heard that tin-mining was a possibility again in Cornwall,' Crow said, 'with the rise in tin prices, but in Devon—'

'No, it's not tin-mining I'm talking about — though as you rightly guess I'm concerned with giving you some background to existing operations rather than a history lesson. The fact is, in 1867 some character called Nicholls discovered a mineral called wolframite in Dartmoor granite.'

'And?'

'Wolframite contains tungsten. It is,' Gray added drily, 'an iron manganese tungstate, grey black in colour, with a shiny metallic lustre on cleavage faces. Or so I'm told.'

'I'll take your word for it.' They left the park and crossed the road at a run, avoiding the heavy mid-morning traffic. 'I imagine our meeting this morning will be something to do with wolframite?'

'In a manner of speaking. I'm just giving you background, as I said, in case we get jargon thrown at us. We're going to meet Edward Foster, the Minister for Development and Exploration, and, coincidentally enough, MP for the area in question as well. And with him, I understand, will be the head of an American exploration company.'

'I don't think that five minutes' talk with you about wolframite and tungsten, and a *very* potted history of the Devon mining industry, is going to equip me adequately for a discussion with a Minister and an American big wheel,' Crow complained.

'Ah, but your function will not be to evaluate either the political situation or the tungsten-bearing properties of the place in question. Your function will be much more in line with your talents.'

'My function?'

'They want you to find out who murdered their Environmental Coordinator.'

'Their *what?*'

'His name,' Commander Gray said as he led the way up the steps, 'was Fred Norman.'

* * *

Edward Foster was tall, slim and confident; he had the air of a heavily insured man, and seemed to be constantly smiling; the lift of the corners of his mouth was disarming, so that the most biting remark would have its edge removed, even though its sharpness would remain and cut deep. He was immaculately suited, carefully groomed, with his long, waving hair neatly brushed back from his forehead. His office matched his own appearance: up to date, gleaming, and efficient. The chairs were deep and leather-covered, and the furnishings expensive, for apart from his life as a politician, Foster had family money and a family business of consequence behind him. He could *afford* politics, in a way others could not. He greeted Gray and Crow cordially, waved them to chairs, and offered them drinks in a manner that it would have been churlish to refuse.

'I'm grateful that you could come, gentlemen,' Foster said. 'Mr Streisman should be with us in a few minutes: his secretary just phoned to say he was on the way. You . . . er . . . you're familiar with Mr Streisman's background, by the way?'

Crow glanced at Gray, and then shook his head. 'I'm afraid I know nothing of him.'

'Ah well, perhaps I should say a few words, then,' Foster said smoothly. 'First of all, he's a Mormon, and a strict one at that.' He paused, eyeing the drink in his hand. 'I should add, perhaps, that his Mormonism does not extend to an outright condemnation of social activities such as drinking — though he himself drinks only water and lemonade and other non-alcoholic drinks — but he does insist on what may be called the . . . ah . . . old-fashioned virtues in his business activities. Don't get me wrong — he has a reputation for ruthlessness and hard bargaining, but he does not get involved in what may be described as shady practices, and he demands a scrupulous honesty in his subordinates. He is also . . . a man in a hurry.'

'A young man?' Crow queried.

'No. You misunderstand. He is in his sixties now, but has no great desire to meet his Maker. No, he has an energy that demands the constant expansion of his interests, and leaves one with the impression that he is in a rush to get everything done while it's there to get done.'

Ten minutes later Crow realized what Foster had meant, when Mr Myron Streisman surged into the room and was introduced. He was a small, restless man, built like a rubber ball, and seemingly possessing many of its properties. He did not sit, but moved around the room while they talked, and his bright, narrow-spaced eyes were never still, flickering glances weighted with calculation at each of his companions; a business mathematician weighing up the chances of profit from each of the men in the room. He had, apparently, built up a supermarket empire in the States before he was forty, but of recent years he had turned first to light industry, and then to the more exciting field of exploration.

'And it *is* exciting, gentlemen,' he insisted in his rasping, rather strident tone. 'It fulfils the pioneering spirit in all of us. The challenge of seeking out new deposits, of making the land work for us, spill out its treasures, maybe opening up new horizons — it's more than exciting, it's the touchstone, the philosopher's dream in some ways — the metamorphosis of fantasy into reality. That's my business, and that's my dream.'

'We all have our dreams,' Foster said, smiling, 'and many of mine are rooted in my constituency, as well as my Department of State. In this instance, yours and mine coincide very clearly. You see, Superintendent Crow, Streisman Exploration Incorporated has entered into certain agreements to carry out feasibility studies to determine whether it's possible to produce tungsten by a mining and crushing process — and if it's successful it could be important for England's future.'

'You may not know it,' Streisman interrupted, 'but half of the world supply is mined in China, Russia and North Korea. We mine it in the States, too, but it could well be that the Ottershaw deposits in Devon — provided they can be mined commercially — could be a significant economic asset to the UK. There's already a small mine in the Lake District — but we're talking here of a production of between two and ten million pounds of tungsten a year. And that means carbide for cutting tools, high-speed die steels and super alloys, pure metal products such as electrodes, cathodes, filaments, bulbs, and a whole range of chemicals and compounds for non-metallurgical applications. But it's the carbides and wear-resistant materials that will be the most important product—'

'And apart from that,' Foster interrupted in his turn, 'the Ottershaw operation could lead to the employment of some three hundred men in an area which has a fairly high unemployment rate.'

And jobs mean votes, John Crow thought to himself. 'How long has your company been working at Ottershaw?' he asked.

Streisman paced nervously around the room, swivelling his small bullet head to keep his glance fixed on John Crow. 'Two years now, and we've moved fast. We've carried out an extensive drilling programme which shows reserves of maybe fifty-five million tonnes of low-concentrate mineral-bearing rock in a granite block. It's part of a feasibility study that's cost us three million pounds already, and we're prepared to spend another five million, maybe seven million, during the next two years.'

'And that's before you produce any ore?' Crow asked in surprise.

'You got to put money in to get money out,' Streisman said a trifle impatiently.

'I think,' Commander Gray remarked, 'the details of the Ottershaw operation could more conveniently be given to Detective Superintendent Crow in the dossier that's been prepared for him. And I believe the Project Manager will be available to talk to him in due course?'

'That's right.' Streisman nodded emphatically. 'He's in London right now, and they can talk when they go down to Devon together.'

John Crow glanced quickly at Commander Gray, but the pipe was out and the eyes averted. He turned back to Foster and Streisman.

'You talk of my going down to Devon,' he said in a quiet tone.

'That's right,' Foster said quickly, before Streisman could answer. 'You see, there's been a bit of trouble down there.'

'I'll say there's been trouble!' Streisman exploded, unwilling to be excluded by Foster's politician smoothness. 'I tell you, Crow, we've sunk so much damn money into this project, and yet we seem to meet nothing but problems! The reason why I'm over here in Europe is that I'm making a whistle-stop tour of all our operations; I was in Brussels yesterday and flew in last night just for this meeting. I'm not *due* here, dammit, for a couple of weeks, when we have the official opening of the plant at Ottershaw, but I thought I'd better come over to make sure things were going right. Trouble, you say? Too much damn trouble — and it's ended with Fred Norman getting himself killed!'

Edward Foster cleared his throat with a delicate cough.

He smiled deprecatingly. 'The situation, Superintendent, is that in carrying out the feasibility study, our American friends have met a certain . . . ah . . . opposition, even though they have been taking the utmost pains to avoid trouble, and indeed prevent it arising. In my view, the company is a model in the way it has attempted to forestall all possible objections to open-pit mining in the area of Ottershaw.'

'You mean there has been environmental opposition?' Crow asked.

'Not exactly. As a true politician,' Foster said, smiling, 'I must say, yes and no. The *potential* for opposition exists, of course, but its main bite has been lessened by the great work that the company has done to prevent issues arising. But all this the Project Manager can explain to you. We should perhaps concentrate on this man Norman.'

'He was found dead,' Myron Streisman rasped. 'His body surfaced from the sludge in the tailings pond about a month ago. At first they thought it was suicide, but that was nonsense. Murder. He was *murdered.* And we want you to sort the thing out. I tell you, in the tailings pond of the plant, before we open the blasted place! We couldn't get worse publicity!'

John Crow was beginning to take a dislike to Myron Streisman. 'You want me to . . . sort this out. I'm afraid you've got things wrong, somehow.' He glanced in Gray's direction, but the Commander's head was still averted. 'You see, I've had no instruction that the services of Scotland Yard are required at Ottershaw. The Murder Squad has received no request.'

'We're making it now,' Streisman said, his eyebrows rising at what he clearly saw as stupidity in John Crow.

'No,' Crow replied. 'You misunderstand. The *local* force has made no request, to my knowledge—'

'But that's the damn point,' Streisman said angrily. 'They won't make a request; they won't get off their fat butts long enough to scratch—'

'I don't think we need go into that,' Foster interposed swiftly as he saw John Crow's mouth harden. 'Let me assure you, Superintendent, there will be no problem—'

'I can't accept such a bald assurance, Mr Foster. As Commander Gray knows, the procedural arrangements in these cases are clear. If a crime is committed within the bailiwick of a local force, that force handles it. The services of the Murder Squad are called upon only if that local force makes the request. Such forces are, quite rightly in my view, often reluctant to make such a call. Their own local knowledge, their own developed expertise, their own understanding of the area—'

'But they're damned incompetent,' Streisman snapped. 'And I came over here to get things moving. We can't afford to let things hang fire.'

He was staring at Edward Foster as he spoke, and the politician was aware of the hostility in the glance. He turned his insincere smile on John Crow. 'You must understand, Superintendent, just how important this issue is. Factually, we owe a great deal to Mr Streisman and his company, both for the solid investment already made, and for the jobs he is bringing to the area. Moreover, I need make no mention of the massive potential of the site at Ottershaw and the industrial independence it will possibly give us in certain areas. We simply cannot afford to let anything go wrong in this matter.'

'And a local murder investigation is going to damage that?' Crow asked in disbelief.

'You haven't got it clear,' Streisman said, walking forward angrily. 'You say a murder, okay, that's it. But all my life I've worked on instinct in business, and my instinct tells me there's something wrong at Ottershaw. The opposition, all right, it's not been too well orchestrated, but something *smells* down there, something in *my* operation, and I won't stand for that. The murder, for me, that's just the tip of an iceberg. I wanna know what's going on there — and I'll bet my reputation that it's got something to do with Norman's killing!'

'You mean you want me to carry out some kind of investigation into company matters as well?' Crow asked in surprise.

'It'll be the same damned thing,' Myron Streisman said, glowering. 'It's all tied in. Pick out the rat, and the whole pack will emerge.'

Edward Foster licked his lips carefully. 'We, well, we don't exactly feel precisely the way Mr Streisman does, but Ottershaw *is* of vital importance, and Mr Streisman feels central expert investigatory power should be applied to the problem. We were told you'd be the best man for the job.'

'But that's not how things *work*,' Crow insisted.

'It's how they're going to work this time,' Commander Gray said in a quiet but firm tone. Crow paused, then turned to look at him. Gray met his glance directly. 'I'm sorry, John, but that's how it is.'

'It's precisely how it is,' Foster remarked. 'This is top level, Crow; an instruction has gone out to the Commissioner—'

John Crow ignored him. 'You know what this means,' he said to Gray.

'You've no choice, John, and neither have I. So we'll be putting you on the train in two days. You'll be in charge of the investigation into the murder of Fred Norman.'

Edward Foster was frowning, and the corners of his mouth no longer displayed the smiling lift they customarily carried. His tone had become icy. 'I'm not sure I approve of this prima donna approach of yours, Crow. What the hell does it matter to you how you're called in to this case? Do you object to working in the government interest, in the local interest, or is it just that you don't like working in the interests of big business?'

John Crow turned to the politician, his eyes burning. 'You know your business, Mr Foster, and I know mine. Commander Gray will be able to tell you about my objections — maybe he already has, but just in case he hasn't, I'll give them to you and Mr Streisman right now. A local force has pride in its men and its methods. It has its finger on all sorts of pulses that an outsider can't reach. And if an *unwelcome* outsider comes in, fingers get removed from pulses.'

'Are you suggesting the local force would refuse to cooperate?' Foster demanded.

Crow shook his head. 'Not openly. But human nature being what it is, the locals will see this as a huge slight upon their own integrity and competence. They'll cooperate, but with an understandable reluctance — and that can be the kiss of death to an operation. You should wait for the request—'

'We can't wait!' Myron Streisman said emphatically. 'I want this cleared up before the opening of the plant, and before I have to return Stateside. Those local hicks will never clear it up; I want Scotland Yard involved. I'm told that's you . . .' His little eyes had narrowed, as he weighed up Crow again, overriding the anger of the last few minutes. He nodded, as though accepting Crow's interpretation of the difficulties of the situation. 'And I think I've been told right. I want you down there, Superintendent Crow.'

And what Myron Streisman wanted, John Crow thought wearily, as he heard no dissent from Foster or Gray, Myron Streisman always got.

* * *

Commander Gray and John Crow walked back through St James's Park, both men largely preoccupied with their own thoughts. Gray knew how Crow was feeling, and was aware of a certain sympathy in his own veins for Crow's attitude, but it was something he was in no position to act upon. He had his job to do, also. Crow paused as they reached the bridge and Gray halted.

'You know what it's going to be like, don't you?' Crow asked bitterly. 'Worse than it ever is. Local resentment is bound to surface; there'll be obstacles placed in my way. They'll not want to see an outsider come in and do their job.'

'They've already protested, John.'

'But they'll go along with it?'

'They have to. The Chief Constable all but blew a fuse, but Foster has some pull and, well . . .'

Above them in the blue sky a silent jet gleamed silver, a vapour trail wisping from its tail. Crow watched it until it had disappeared, and then he looked at Bill Gray. 'All right. I suppose I've got no choice either. But I want some sound support; a man I can trust.'

'You name him.'

'There's a young man recently joined us. A graduate called Delaval. I want him.'

'Detective Inspector . . . the youngster you worked with up north recently?'

'That's him.' Crow frowned. 'He's got flair; we make a good team. And I've got the feeling that it'll need more than just perseverance to satisfy Myron Streisman.'

'Delaval . . .' Bill Gray nodded, and resumed the walk across the park. 'All right, John, you've got him. He'll be travelling south-west with you in two days.'

* * *

John Crow found it difficult to stay awake on trains. It was constitutional, his wife Martha told him; something in his make-up that made him close his eyes, in the same way that he did whenever she wanted to raise some particularly important domestic issue with him, like papering the sitting-room before Christmas. And he dozed now, for twenty minutes or so after the train pulled out on the journey to Exeter. His sleep was disturbed thereafter, however, by Delaval's return with a cup of coffee that he had fetched for himself from the buffet car.

'Sorry . . . You want one?'

Crow shook his head and yawned. 'No, thanks. I can manage until we get to Exeter. Any sign of this man Grainger?'

Detective Inspector Delaval nodded. 'He was in a reserved seat in carriage C. I explained you wanted to do some . . . er . . . work before you had a chat with him and he said that was all right.' He grinned conspiratorially. 'You done enough work now?'

'Mind your manners, young man.' Crow glanced out of the window at the countryside flowing past as the train hurtled south-west. 'I see no reason why we have to plunge into this case immediately. Give me the benefit of an hour's rest from business, at least.'

'Grainger seemed in no hurry to meet *you*, either.'

Crow glanced at Delaval. He was a good-looking young man, almost thirty now, with fair hair that was sufficiently wayward to give him the appearance of being even younger. His boyish looks were added to by a gentleness about his mouth that Crow knew belied the steel in the man; Delaval's blue eyes gave a better clue to his character, for they were full of cold light, the kind that anger could harden in a way that would leave a woman scared and a man nervous. Crow had first worked with him in Newcastle; since that occasion, Delaval, uneasy at the attitudes adopted towards him in his northern force, had obtained a transfer to the Met and an attachment to the Murder Squad. Crow had known of his coming and his reasons for it: Delaval still felt he had to live down the fact that he was a graduate entrant with colleagues who had come in with a different background and more traditional qualifications. This was the first time Crow had sought the support of Delaval since his transfer. But he was aware of his strengths and, perhaps more important, his weaknesses. He guessed Delaval's impetuosity had not been completely lost — it would be still allied to his flair — but the man's reading of character would have become more careful, particularly after the unprofessional involvement he had succumbed to in the Sweet murder up north, and he had qualities that Crow wanted, and could use, in support on this case.

'So what's your impression of Grainger, then?'

Delaval removed the top of the plastic cup and tasted the coffee, grimacing, before he replied. 'About forty, I'd have said. Is that young for a Project Manager on this kind of job? I wouldn't know, really. Ahhh . . . now then . . . thickset, about five-ten, sort of face you'd expect to see on a boxer, you know? Sort of squashed by too much punching. But he's got kind of *earnest* eyes that I don't believe in—'

'You'll have to explain that to me,' Crow interrupted.

'They tell me he wants to be helpful and will give me any information I want to know. But I don't believe them. I think when he raises his eyebrows — they're rather thick, by the way, and meet in the middle — it's with the idea he's injecting sincerity into his glance, and I don't trust that kind of . . . er . . . projection.'

'Fanciful,' Crow murmured.

'There's a place for it,' Delaval replied meaningfully, and Crow smiled. Delaval was as aware of John Crow's weaknesses as Crow was of Delaval's: there had been times, including the Newcastle case, when Crow himself had gone for intuition rather than fact. If only Martha knew . . . He must take this young man home with him some time. Abruptly he rose to his feet. 'All right, finish your coffee and then come on down to join us. I'll go make myself known to our friend Grainger.'

The description Delaval had given John Crow was accurate, but he had not mentioned the firmness of Grainger's grip, nor the charm of the smile the man could give. When Crow introduced himself, Grainger rose and greeted him warmly, then slid to the inside seat to make room for the policeman.

'Is Inspector Delaval joining us?'

'He'll be along in a few minutes,' Crow replied. 'Did your conference in London go well?'

'Well enough. The others are staying on to tie up some loose ends, but we can't afford to keep all the senior staff away from Ottershaw for too long at once.'

'So who's left in London, then?'

Grainger smiled, and fingered his lower lip with a stubby forefinger. 'The rest of the team, really: Pete Harris, the Exploration Manager; John Wood, the Senior Metallurgist; Ted Nicholas, the Mineralogist — and O'Connor, the new . . . the new Environmental Coordinator.'

The replacement for Fred Norman, the man found dead in the tailings pond at the new plant in Ottershaw.

Both men were silent for a few minutes, and then Crow asked, 'Did you know Norman very well?'

Grainger shook his head. 'Not really. Fred kept pretty much to himself — rarely saw much of him outside working hours. Though for that matter . . .' Grainger glanced at Crow, and gave an apologetic smile. 'I think you'll find that as a working team we're a pretty queer bunch.'

'How do you mean?'

'Difficult to explain, really. I suppose it stems essentially from Myron Streisman — he appointed each of us personally, you know, and I suspect there are certain qualities in each of us that gave us our jobs. The same kind of qualities, I mean.'

'Such as?'

'Commitment.'

'That's surely always the kind of quality an employer is looking for,' Crow suggested.

'Ah yes, but . . .' Grainger hesitated for a moment, and then went on, 'Pete Harris is single, and single-minded. He's passionately concerned that the feasibility studies we're undertaking should produce the answers we're looking for. This job is a big breakthrough for him — he's only twenty-eight. Me, I'm divorced, and my world tends to be within the boundaries of Ottershaw. Ted Nicholas, well, I gather he's got the kind of marital arrangement that makes no demands on him, so he rarely visits his wife in Dorset. We're not alone as a group — there are others, too . . . It just makes me suspect that when Myron makes his appointments it's on the basis that celibacy is next to godliness. Perhaps he hopes that our personal needs in certain directions will be sublimated by the work we do.'

'Are they?'

Grainger looked away. 'We're almost always on site, I can tell you that.'

Delaval slid into the seat opposite them, and nodded to Grainger. Crow thought it time to move away from the interesting but probably irrelevant thesis Grainger was propounding, to matters of more moment. 'I think, Mr Grainger, it would be useful if you could develop a little more of the background to the Ottershaw operation for us. And then we can talk a bit more about Fred Norman.'

Grainger nodded, and immediately launched, with a familiarity that showed he was well accustomed to the task, into an explanation of what Streisman was doing and hoped to achieve at the Ottershaw site in Devon. He explained that the operation was still in the initial stages, with feasibility studies being undertaken to the extent of perhaps eight million pounds. Though they had located a deposit of mineral-bearing rock, the concentration of tungsten — bearing material was low.

'That's why we've now built the pilot plant at Ottershaw,' Grainger went on. 'Once the mineralized material has been mined it will be crushed, and then the plant will test laboratory recovery processes to determine whether they can be scaled up to a full commercial operation. Many of these processes are as yet untried.'

'What about the mining methods to be used?' Delaval asked.

'Open-pit,' Grainger replied. 'Got to be. And that's where the problems start, obviously.'

'Obviously?'

Grainger's eyes were as sincere as Delaval had predicted. 'The aim of the project is not only to discover whether mining the tungsten is commercially feasible; we have to find out if it's environmentally feasible as well. Ottershaw is an *environmentally* sensitive area.'

Crow enjoyed the delicacy of the description. 'That's why it was necessary to appoint an Environmental Coordinator?'

'That's right. It's a major part of the study, and takes cognizance of all the basic elements in the proposed mining programme. The open-pit mine, the problems of handling and disposal of large waste tonnages must be looked at carefully; we're doing field studies to quantify dust deposition; we're analysing the range of chemical parameters in two streams; we're making an inventory of plant and animal communities . . .'

'You're taking it all very seriously,' Crow said.

'In spite of there being no *legal* necessity for it, Myron Streisman believes a detailed examination of the environmental implications of the Ottershaw project is necessary.'

'He also believes,' Crow said mildly, 'that the work is bedevilled by rather too many problems.'

For just a moment the sincerity vanished from Grainger's eyes to be replaced by some other, deep-seated, more naked emotion. Then he looked away, out over the fields under the hazy sun. 'There are problems, certainly. Most of them inevitable.'

'Such as?'

Grainger glanced towards Delaval, then turned again to Crow. 'They're company problems,' he said brusquely, 'and I don't think you need to bother with them. You're interested only in Fred Norman's death, and I wouldn't want to waste your time.'

Crow smiled. 'Ah well, that's as may be. It's possible the problems *could* be of interest, but no matter, for now. Let's stick perhaps just to those . . . ah . . . company problems that might have had relation to the dead man.'

Grainger pulled a face, then nodded. 'All right. I'd better say, right off, that Fred Norman's job was of the kind that deserved every penny he was being paid. He got a fair bit of hassle, and it was building up. Quite apart from all the monitoring he had to do of the field studies, he also had to take steps to mitigate or prevent potential problems. And a few of these have been brewing.'

'What did they comprise?' Delaval asked.

'The obvious ones, I suppose. Pollution, to start with. I think Fred more or less had that one in hand. But he was being less successful over the transport problem. When you come out to the site, as you will, I suppose—'

'Today,' Crow said firmly. 'just to take an early look at the plant and the tailings pond.'

'Okay.' Grainger nodded. 'Well, you can talk to Alan Fairfield, our Transport Manager. He'd been working with Fred over the lorries problem in Ottershaw: he'll be able to explain that problem. And then there's Brigadier Leveson, who's gone back on some agreements that Fred had reached with him over conduit rights and a projected roadway. And then there are the planning enquiries that have got bogged down. I suppose, apart from various minor issues, those were the headaches Fred Norman had.'

'And do you consider any of them might have made some contribution to his death?'

Grainger's eyes were steady as he held Crow's glance. 'I've no idea why Fred Norman died, but I'm convinced it had nothing to do with any company activity.'

Crow nodded, and was silent for a while. At last he asked, 'What sort of man was Fred Norman?'

'I can't say I knew him *very* well,' Grainger replied. 'As I told you, he kept pretty well to himself outside working hours. But he was a good man: a biologist by trade, so to speak, about fifty years old. His wife died some years back and they had no children; I got the impression that after that he became completely committed to his work — in the Myron Streisman mould again, you see. He'd been working for the company for about . . . oh, I'd say, seven or eight years. First in the States, then latterly at Ottershaw.'

'Did he live near the site?'

Grainger nodded. 'Not far from the village. He'd bought a small cottage on the edge of the moor; lived there alone and looked after himself. A tidy man: I was only there the once, but everything was neat as a new pin; everything in place; it was almost as though each item was ticketed for sale, you know? There weren't tickets there, of course — but it all looked so . . . *neat.*'

'Was he that kind of man in his work?' Delaval asked. Grainger scratched his chin thoughtfully and stared out of the window for a few seconds: moorhens whirred across a canal as the train sped past, and the placid surface of the water was scarred by their scuttering feet. 'Well,' Grainger said, 'he was . . . but . . . oh, I hesitate, because lately I felt his attitudes towards his work had changed.'

'How do you mean?' Crow pressed.

Grainger made a vague fluttering movement with his hand. 'Don't get me wrong. Fred was a sound man; a hard worker, and he was doing a damn good job on the feasibility study. You'll see some of his work at the site and you'll understand what I mean. But, well, maybe it was the way things seemed to be coming to a head, blowing up in his face, if you like, maybe it was that which caused him to become withdrawn . . . morose . . .'

'He was depressed? Because he was under pressure?'

Grainger frowned. 'I don't know. I can't be that . . . er . . . definite, really. All I *can* say is that there was a change in him; he was never the *chattering* kind, but lately, these last couple of months, he became somewhat withdrawn. I put it down to the pressure of work, of course, but now . . .'

'Now?'

Grainger's frown deepened, and his eyes became hazy with doubt. 'Well, he's dead, isn't he? Murdered. It makes you wonder . . .'

'Wonder what?' Crow asked quietly.

Grainger made no reply for a moment. Then he said, 'I don't know that he had any enemies. But . . . but he must have had one, at least.'

And that's all it can take, John Crow thought to himself.

* * *

The three men left the train at Exeter: a company car was waiting, and while they were driven to the Streisman head office in the town, Grainger explained that it would have been more appropriate in many ways to have had the head office in Plymouth, since that city was nearer to Ottershaw site. The reason Exeter had been chosen was that Myron Streisman felt it had a better image: smaller, less cosmopolitan, more 'county', and with a more obvious sense of history, in spite of Drake and Plymouth Hoe. He loved Roman ruins, Grainger added, and it was the sight of the newly-exposed Roman bridge over the River Exe, and its preservation, that had finally decided the matter. So Exeter it was as the Streisman centre.

And that meant a drive over the moor to reach the Ottershaw site.

They took lunch with Grainger. Crow was tempted to place a call to the Chief Constable to tell him of his arrival, but resisted it; there would be time to climb that particular frosty mountain later. He contented himself with a call to his hotel to confirm that he and Delaval would be arriving there in the early evening. That meant they had the afternoon in which to visit the site. Grainger announced he would be happy to take them out to the site, so by two o'clock they were back in the car and heading out of Exeter on the Okehampton Road. Grainger explained that it was faster to take the main road to Plymouth, but he himself preferred the more scenic, if winding, route over Dartmoor.

It was a decision that appealed to Crow; he got little enough opportunity to drive through pleasant countryside, and in the sunlit afternoon he enjoyed the climb into the moor, with Grainger proving himself to be a good guide, pointing out tors and naming them, directing their attention to the tiny combes and streams, and as they drew near Tavistock, showing them the hill sites, the hut circles on White Tor and Launceston Moor.

'And here's the first of the old mines — the Devon Friendship Mine at Marytavy,' he announced. 'I've brought you the long way around to give you a full picture, but now we'll be running direct for Ottershaw, and you'll see that while there are environmental considerations to take into account, they're not as fierce as they could be, in the sense that mining of one kind or another has already scarred the landscape.'

A little while later Crow and Delaval saw what he meant, as the grey-white heaps of china-clay waste lifted their peaks from the surrounding moor, and they left the straggling streams under the hill to climb towards the wooded slope.

As they passed over a long, looping road that ran beside a thickly wooded area flanked by pastureland, Crow asked whom the estate belonged to.

'Brigadier Leveson,' Grainger replied. 'One of the thorns in our side. We thought Fred Norman had it all buttoned up, but in some way or another he and Leveson got at cross purposes, Leveson pulled out of the fixed agreements, and now the whole damned thing is bogged down in a planning enquiry. The Brigadier, one might say, is being less than helpful.'

The road curved, cutting a little way through the trees, and then Crow caught sight of the sign which proclaimed that Ottershaw was just four miles distant.

'We'll go down through the village and then swing left on the company track that takes us up to the plant. You see, if only Leveson would cooperate we'd drive a road on the west side of that hill there, which would bypass the village of Ottershaw, cut across that shoulder through the trees, and come out about half a mile from the plant. But . . . I don't know what went wrong with him and Fred Norman, but something did.' He hesitated. 'And Leveson's intransigence causes — or at least exacerbates — other problems.'

'Such as?'

'I expect you'll see, in a moment,' Grainger said grimly.

And when they entered the outskirts of Ottershaw, Crow and Delaval saw what he meant.

* * *

The road ran almost straight for perhaps two hundred yards, dipping from the hill between the narrow sides of the combe towards the village of Ottershaw itself. Trees clustered on the sides of the combe, and scattered cottages lined the hill, nestling among the trees, but the village itself was almost a ribbon development along the main road that ran through its length. At the entrance to the combe there were cottages flanking the roadside, each neat and tidy, with painted fences and well-controlled, pocket-handkerchief front gardens. Beyond them was the main street itself, with a scattering of small shops, a public house, and a tiny chapel. Beyond that, Crow could not see, as the car slowed and stopped.

The roadway was blocked.

It had been simply done. Crow got out with Delaval, at Grainger's suggestion, and observed the problem. Outside the grocer's store a small van was drawn up: apparently it was owned by the grocer himself. Some thirty yards beyond the van, and on the same side of the road, a car was parked, while on the opposite pavement, placed between these two vehicles, there was a baker's van. Two lorries stood discharging unwelcome fumes from their exhausts as they waited for one of the vehicles to move, for they effectively prevented any other vehicle from passing along the road; one lorry-driver was leaning from his cab, exchanging obscenities with a man standing near the car. Neither seemed committed to the conversation: it was as though they were carrying out some routine, well-rehearsed play-acting. The words were violent, the gestures contemptuous, but both men seemed to know nothing would come of them.

Crow and Delaval stood watching them for a few minutes: the man standing beside the car was of middle height, and perhaps thirty years of age. He wore a donkey jacket, and his shoulders filled the jacket powerfully. His hair was black, cut short, and his heavy eyebrows were ridged angrily as he shouted back at the lorry-driver leaning from his cab. His fists were clenched, but his hands were at his sides, and there was no leaning towards violence, though Crow guessed that this would be a man to whom violence would not be foreign.

'Should we . . . er . . . interfere?' Delaval asked doubtfully.

Crow shook his head. 'I think not. This is almost a ritual, it seems to me. They'll withdraw in a moment or so, one way or another.'

Even as he spoke, a woman emerged from a general store across the road and some fifty metres down the street. She walked casually towards the car. Her hair was long and auburn, her mouth a red, discontented gash, her eyes wide and bold. She wore a white sweater that outlined her breasts, and tight corduroy slacks that enabled her to mince along in an entirely provocative manner. The lorry-driver saw her coming and shouted something to her: she raised one hand with fingers extended in a gesture of obscene defiance. The man beside the car turned and got into the car, opening the door for her from the inside: she took the driving seat, and a few minutes later the car pulled away down the street in the same direction as the lorry was facing. Cursing, the lorry-driver ground his gears and inched his heavy vehicle forward, negotiating the tight space between the parked vans with difficulty. The grocer stood just inside his doorway, watching. He made no attempt to ease the problem by moving his van.

The second lorry followed the first. There was the sharp smell of exhaust fumes in the air, and a fine layer of white dust drifted behind the tailboard of the second lorry. Crow heard another lorry coming down the hill, and he turned and walked with Delaval back towards the car in which Grainger waited with a resigned look in his eyes.

'Police?' Crow asked.

Grainger opened the door for the two detectives. 'They take action once in a while, but this happens every day. It's quite deliberate, as you might have gathered.'

'That's right. They've been through the charade a number of times, that's clear.'

'Ahuh. The fact is, there's a campaign being mounted to try to close the street to heavy traffic, but the problem is that if the china-clay firms can't use Ottershaw road it will mean something like a twenty-mile detour. It's just not practicable. It landed on Fred Norman's plate, of course, in that once the plant opens up, inevitably we'll have a larger number of lorries of our own coming through the village. That means even more trouble — and though he was meeting it in advance, well, things were beginning . . . *are* beginning to blow there too. If Leveson would let us drive west of the hill, of course . . . but the old bastard won't at the moment, and there's an end to it, unless we can persuade the planning authority it's necessary. Even then, a compulsory purchase order would be needed, and the Brigadier has too much pull in the county for that to become other than a remote possibility.'

'How closely involved was Norman with this village problem?' Crow asked.

'It was on his desk,' Grainger replied shortly.

'But your firm's involvement is exacerbating rather than creating the problem,' Delaval said.

'That's right,' Grainger replied, starting the car and easing it forward once the china-clay lorry had rumbled past them, 'but those firms have got enough troubles of their own. They can claim usage and practice — which means damn all, but sounds good — and they'll give us no support at any hearings. They just don't want to know: and I can't say I blame them.'

Delaval glanced at Crow. 'But I got the impression that Streisman had tried to head off all such problems, and was behaving very responsibly on such environmental matters.' He paused, frowning at Grainger. 'So how come the company didn't envisage this difficulty before it even started building the plant at Ottershaw?'

Grainger drove between the parked vans and then increased speed down the main street until the road curved out of the village and began to climb into the hill beyond. 'Let's just say at this stage that we didn't perceive it as a real problem, since our plans envisaged the road on the Leveson estate. But now . . . anyway, from the top of the hill you'll get your first view of the pilot plant.'

In the far distance the line of the Dartmoor hills rose, scarred in places by the white spoil-heaps that shone in the sunlight. Closer, there were scattered farms, copses of trees, and then the road looping over the near hills and leading towards the shoulder under which lay the pilot plant and its scattered buildings, the earth marked redly by the track torn by the company from the main road and leading on to the site itself. As they ran forward in the car and took the company track, Grainger pointed out the main buildings to the two detectives: on the left, a solid-waste disposal area; directly ahead of them the primary crusher and the secondary crushing, washing and sampling plant, and then a little way off to the right, some long, low buildings which Grainger described as the workshop area, which housed laboratory-type equipment.

Behind the workshop was a single-storey building from which a conveyor ran upwards to a larger, two-storey construction. 'The building on the left,' Grainger explained, 'is the sample storage area. When we've mined and crushed the samples they're kept there, before they're run up through the conveyor feed to the pilot plant itself. That's the larger building you can see there.' He pulled the car into a small parking bay just outside the workshop area, and the three men got out. Grainger led the way towards the pilot plant, walking under the feed conveyor ahead of the two detectives.

'As you'll see, we're having to shore up and buttress that slope up there as we're getting some earth movements. And, aware as ever of environmental considerations,' he added, 'we've preserved as much of the existing vegetation cover as we've been able to — it makes no great impact here on the site, but from the hill it breaks up the nakedness of the site itself, and makes it more amenable to the eye. In addition, if we find the feasibility study flops, well, it won't be so difficult to reverse the spoliation if we keep some of the ground cover at least.'

Crow was staring at a number of prefabricated huts of some antiquity, clustered in a huddled group to the side of the sample storage area. 'What are those?'

'Ah well,' Grainger said, wrinkling his nose, 'you must remember this isn't a *new* site. I mean, you see those ruins over there, and that broken-down stack? That's where the old workings are. The Carter Syndicate took up the lease in the mid-thirties and carried out an underground exploration programme.'

'Too late in the day?' Crow suggested.

'That's it. They didn't start until late 1943. When they began, supplies of tungsten were plentiful, the price was low — and so the plant never reached its proper capacity. They tried again later but the equipment had degenerated so much that it was useless. When Mr Streisman took over in the sixties he razed the site, except for those old huts.'

'How come it's only recently that Myron Streisman has developed the site?' Crow asked.

Grainger smiled thinly. 'He's a wily old bird. He really took on the lease as a loss-leader, a tax avoidance device. But when the prices began to look right, he knew he was going to be able to develop things — if the feasibility study worked out. One way, he'll make a mint; the other, he can still count it against tax if it's a dead loss. And, of course, with the arrangement he's come to with the Government, through Foster, he's on a pretty good wicket.' He shook his head. 'It's my guess that the Carter group, if there are any of them still around, will be kicking themselves that *they* didn't show the kind of entrepreneurial skills that old Myron has.'

Grainger led the way past the drilling rig, which, he explained, had to be a diamond operation, since the tungsten had to be extracted from granite, like a china-clay deposit, and described its technical data with a hint of pride that suggested to Crow that Grainger might originally have been a drilling man himself. He certainly seemed to enjoy describing the Boyles BBS 56 diamond drill, trailer-mounted, with its raking mast equipment allowing for 30-metre rod-pulls. Crow caught Delaval's eye and smiled: every man should have his own professional passion, he thought.

'Where exactly is the tailings pond where Norman's body was found?' he asked.

Grainger raised a hand, pointing. 'If we go past those old spoil-heaps, beyond the trenches, we'll come to it. You see the hoist engine-house?' He indicated a low building some twenty feet high. 'We'll take that track there, and cut across to the left. It's the disposal area for mine water and tailings. Not a particularly attractive site.'

Crow was inclined to agree with Grainger when they had walked across and finally stood beside the tailings pond. It was perhaps sixty yards long and thirty wide, a depression filled with grey, murky water and sludge, its surface thickened with scum, its edges still and slimy with black mud. From the tailings pond itself Crow could look back at the site, and in front of him rose the hill above Ottershaw village, perhaps four miles distant from this spot. He glanced about him to the roadway and the company track scarring the red earth, and he considered the situation silently for a few minutes.

'Do you know exactly where the body was found?' he asked at last.

'Near as dammit,' Grainger replied, 'the far corner, over there. It's the deepest section of the pond, and the body should really have sunk, but it must have got caught up on debris beneath the surface. Anyway, one of the drillers saw the head from the rig. He came over, and there was Fred Norman.'

'Any theories as to how he was brought here?' Delaval asked.

Grainger shrugged. 'That's police business, not mine. But there's only one way, I suppose, if it was done under cover of darkness, as I imagine it would have to be. There are lights burning here at night, and watchmen patrol fairly regularly. If Fred was killed off the site — and the local coppers seem to think that's what happened — a car could have been driven up from the main road, along the southern track, just below the hilltop. You can't see the track from the site because of the contour of the land, but see where it comes out, just a matter of fifty yards from the hoist engine-house? If the car was parked there, Fred's body could have been dragged or carried the rest of the way to the pond's edge. To sink without trace. Except it didn't.'

'Were any pieces of evidence found to support that theory?' Crow asked.

'You'll have to ask your colleagues that,' Grainger replied. 'I'm not in their confidence. But there was some talk going around that they'd found track marks beside the engine-house — though that could have been anything, in my view. I mean, lorries and other vehicles are always trundling up around there. And Pete Harris was telling me that he'd heard they found scuff marks, which suggested a body had been dragged along. But evidence of that kind, on a site like this?' The Project Manager shook his head scornfully. 'I don't credit it. This is an industrial site. That kind of evidence would be tough to come by, if you ask me.'

'Hmmm.' Crow looked about him again. 'That overhead cable?'

'South West Electricity Board power cable.'

'It supplies power to the site. And here we are on the what . . . eastern perimeter of the site?'

'That's right.'

Crow calculated the distance with his eye. 'What do you think, Delaval? The lights strung along there . . . fifty yards?'

'I'd say about that,' Delaval replied carefully.

'I doubt whether they'd supply much illumination to the tailings pond,' Crow commented.

A short silence fell, in which Grainger glanced from one man to the other and then fell into an uneasy contemplation of the murky surface of the tailings pond. When Crow spoke again Grainger started, and his eyes were watchful and nervous.

'You said you considered Norman's murder had nothing to do with company matters,' Crow said.

'That's my opinion.'

'But I think you'd agree it has *some* connection with the company?'

'In what way? I don't see—'

'The lights,' Crow said. 'They don't illuminate the tailings pond. The road beyond the engine-house: it's below the hilltop, so again would not be illuminated by the lights. We can *presume,* perhaps, that the man who drove Norman's body up here — if that's what he did do — would not have been so foolish as to use headlights, which might have been noticed, and investigated by the watchman.'

'I think that's fair enough,' Grainger muttered.

'So what can we assume, then?' Crow asked gently. Grainger was not to be drawn. He shrugged, scowled, hunched his shoulders in his jacket, and stared at the tailings pond as though he wished he could drain it there and then and deny thereafter that it had ever existed. 'Perhaps,' Crow said quietly, 'Inspector Delaval can fill the points in for you.'

Delaval cleared his throat. 'It seems pretty obvious. Driving along a hillside track after dark without lights; working with a heavy body over broken ground, trenches, past a spoil-heap, again in the dark; using a place to hide the body which to all intents and purposes *should* have been secure . . . As I said, it seems pretty obvious. Whoever worked under those circumstances must have known the ground, the tailings pond area, the lighting situation, and even, probably, the night watchman's habits and movements, pretty thoroughly.'

'A reasonable hypothesis,' Grainger agreed with reluctance.

'And you still think the murder has nothing to do with the company?' Crow asked.

'There's a difference,' Grainger countered, 'between saying the murderer knew the site well, and that he was concerned with the company.'

'How?'

Grainger ran a nervous hand over his chin and looked about him in a vague desperation. 'Look, do you really know what it's like running a site like this? It's pretty quiet right now, but you can count, what, four lorries? The drilling rig, the plant itself, the construction work that's being undertaken beyond those spoil-heaps, the whole damn feasibility study . . . it all involves men, coming and going, day in, day out. Most of them are employed by Streisman, but a lot are merely sub-contractors.'

'Building industry, you mean?' Delaval asked.

'And lorry-drivers — not our own,' Grainger added, 'but those sub-contracting to the builders. We keep a check of all vehicles coming on site — we weren't stopped because my car is known, but cards are normally produced. Even so, there are always strange faces on site — and some familiar ones are not employed by Streisman. *They* would know the site well enough to be able to do what you're suggesting. And they're nothing to do with the company in the way you're suggesting.'

Delaval's eyes told Crow that Grainger was making a valid point. Crow nodded. 'Is it only construction workers and drivers who are sub-contracted labour on the site?'

Grainger shook his head. 'No, we have a major contracting group concerned with the engineering on the project. The Consultant Engineer is from Craydon Engineering Ltd, and that company employs maybe thirty men on site, on a sub-contracting basis from us. That means the men are on site most of the time.' He hesitated for a few moments. 'And, of course, they'd have been in close contact with Fred Norman some of the time.'

'How do you mean?'

'Much of their work has been in connection with the environmental studies Fred was responsible for. Some of their work has been concerned with geological problems, and in that they've worked with Ted Nicholas and Pete Harris, but most of it *has* been on the other surveys. And that meant Fred was co-ordinating the work.'

'Did Norman's work fall into any kind of pattern?' Delaval asked suddenly.

Grainger appeared confused. 'I don't know what you mean. There was routine work, of course, but a pattern? All I can say is that apart from his routine monitoring activity, he also acted as a sort of trouble-shooter as far as environmental situations were concerned. I mean, the lorry problem, and the dust deposit arguments, whenever they came hard it was Fred Norman's job to sort them out.'

'Was he working on anything in particular before he died?' Delaval persisted.

'Well, I can't tell you that. I *do* know he worked pretty closely with Alan Fairfield, in Transport, and Pete Harris, on exploration matters, in the weeks before he disappeared. But exactly what they were about, I can't be sure. All right, I know I'm Project Manager, but we keep dogs to do the barking, and neither Pete, Alan nor Fred himself came running to me with the problem, if there was one. But Fred Norman's secretary, and maybe his successor, O'Connor, can probably put you right on matters like that.' He hesitated. 'Anyway, that's about the size of things. You've seen the site, and the place where Fred was found. I don't think there's any other information I can give you, unless you've specific questions to ask.'

Crow shook his head. 'No, I think that'll do for now. I'd like to come back and talk to some of the other senior people on the site, but I think that'll do for today. We really ought to get back and check in at our hotel.'

And tomorrow he'd be having his first interview with the Chief Constable. It was not an interview he was looking forward to.

CHAPTER 2

The Chief Constable proved to be a diffident, civilized man, who was simply not prepared to allow an atmosphere of resentment to build up in his office in the presence of Crow and his own senior officers. He contented himself with remarking that it had been 'unfortunate' that procedures should have been so clearly dispensed with, and added that he had been assured by Mr Foster, MP, that no disparagement of his own force was intended. He would, naturally, make every endeavour to ensure that Detective Superintendent Crow was given full assistance in his investigation into the death of Fred Norman.

'You have only to ask,' he said with a quiet dignity.

The same diffidence was not apparent among the senior officers in the plain-clothes branch of the force. They were openly resentful of the high-handed way in which Crow had been thrust among them, and it was obvious within the hour that they had no intention of divulging anything unless Crow made specific requests. It was, he explained to Delaval, to a certain extent understandable, and along the lines of the fears he had expressed to Commander Gray, but it still made life extremely difficult for them both. Nevertheless, he painstakingly interviewed the senior officers who had formed the investigating unit, and drew from them most of the information he could have expected them to obtain during the interval since Norman's death.

After the discussions, and having read the dossiers that had been compiled by the officers, Crow sat with Delaval in the bare office that had been assigned to their use for the duration of the investigation.

'So, what have we got?' Crow mused out loud. 'First, that Fred Norman was rendered unconscious by a blow to the head which *might* have killed him, though there is some reason to suspect he might have died of exposure. Which suggests incarceration of some kind in an open situation. We'll certainly have to talk to Forensic about that.'

'Wouldn't mind a trip to Bristol,' Delaval said. 'Used to know a girl at university who came from Bristol. Solicitor there, now. I could look her up.'

'It seems to me it would be better if *I* went,' Crow remarked drily. 'I wouldn't want to be responsible for any upsetting of the legal profession . . . Now, secondly, the files indicate that it's likely Norman *was* killed elsewhere than at the site, and then brought to the tailings pond by car. The opinion is expressed that he might have been killed at his own cottage and taken from there . . .'

'Though I gather the bloodstains found at the cottage aren't conclusive,' Delaval interrupted. 'His blood, sure, but they could have been occasioned by some other incident.'

Crow nodded. 'The point is taken. But if he *was* killed at his cottage, there is the chance he knew his killer fairly well, at least. However, we'll get back to that later. Let's consider the question why, rather than how he was killed.'

There was a short silence. 'That's where we're stuck, isn't it?' Delaval said. 'Nothing our colleagues had to say, and nothing that appears on file would seem to suggest any motive as such, nor any particular leads that point to one of his fellow employees of Streisman.'

'The famous Myron Streisman seems convinced that the murder is connected with company troubles.' Delaval leaned back in his chair, brushed the lock of fair hair from his eyes and contemplated the ceiling.

'That's all very well, but we don't even know what the company troubles are.' He grimaced. 'Nor does Ray Grainger intend telling us, either. *He,* at least, sees them as irrelevant.'

'And maybe they are, maybe they are.' Crow stared at the files in front of him. 'You know, we're going to be hampered in this case not just by a lack of cooperation from the local coppers. I'm afraid we're going to be somewhat badgered by the theories of Myron Streisman. They're rooted in his mind, and I suppose they've tainted ours. Let's try to remember that, when we get particularly bogged down in some of the fantasies that you at least are likely to come up with.'

'I thought you wanted me along *because* of my fantasies, sir,' Delaval remarked in a mock-humble tone.

'Flair, my boy, not fantasy. And not too much of the former, either. First, there must come all the hard, plodding work that you've shown no great inclination for so far. And we'll begin by going together to take a look at Norman's cottage. After that, maybe, we'll work some more on these files, and then plan our campaign.'

* * *

The cottage was isolated, grey-stoned and grey-slated, crouching under the sweep of the hill at the edge of the towering moor beyond. Rhododendrons masked its entrance, guarding the narrow path that ran to the front door, which was green-painted, with a brass knocker. The brass still shone, testifying to its dead owner's persistence and diligence, and the interior of the cottage bore similar witness.

'I see what Grainger meant,' Delaval said as he walked around the sitting-room and inspected the neatly arranged sideboard, easy chairs, settee and personal effects of the murdered man. 'Spick and span. I suppose that tells us something about Fred Norman.'

'Such as?'

'The likelihood that his professional life will be as well ordered as his personal. That should help, surely.'

'It should. And here he is with his wife.' Crow pointed to the photograph on the mantelpiece. A balding man of perhaps forty, his wife beside him, looking at him and smiling; short, rather dumpy, but adoring. He would have missed her, Crow thought, if she looked at him like that. It would have left a tearing gap in his life, and that gap would have demanded the kind of commitment to his job that Myron Streisman looked for. 'He looks . . . nice.'

He was aware that Delaval was staring at him, surprised. But there was no reason why a man shouldn't betray humanity to his colleagues from time to time. Brusquely Crow said, 'You take a look upstairs. I'll look through these drawers here. I know the locals have been through it all already, but there's no harm in another check.'

It proved unproductive, nevertheless, except for a small notebook in which Fred Norman seemed to have kept some kind of record of his movements. It was not a diary, more a scribbling book, and it interested Crow that it had been started only two months previously, contained various notes and notations that meant nothing to the policeman, and seemed to be connected with his work at Ottershaw. When Delaval came down the stairs, shaking his head, Crow showed him the notebook.

'What do you make of all this?'

Delaval studied the sheets of the notebook and read some of the contents out aloud.

'Cassiterite . . . SnO_2 . . . arsenopyrite . . . What's all this about? Rock grading 0.19% . . . 0.30% Sn . . .' He looked up at Crow, puzzled. 'Greek to me.'

'And me. And what's that table about?' Crow asked. Delaval stared at it. The table was neatly drawn and edged.

B	Percussion diamond	12	1200
C	Reverse Circulation	6	1300
D	Percussion diamond	12	2000
E	Percussion diamond	5	3000

'I haven't the faintest idea. Maybe Grainger can tell us.'

'Mmm. Well, I don't know why the locals didn't pick it up, but I think we'd better hang on to it and have a word with the Ottershaw people about it. Nothing upstairs, then?'

'Nothing. Neat, tidy, sparse, almost spartan. He was no high liver, our friend.'

'Right. Well, let's lock up and leave the place to its ghosts,' Crow said. 'We've got a long evening ahead of us on those files. Excursions are over for the moment — until tomorrow.'

* * *

Hours spent on the files that evening produced nothing of consequence. Before the hotel service ended, Crow called for some drinks to be sent to the residents lounge, and he sprawled there in an easy chair, his long, ungainly legs stretched out in front of him, while he contemplated his younger companion with an air of gloom.

'We're not getting very far, Delaval.'

'Early days, sir.'

'Very early. But I'm not happy on general grounds, you know. The genesis of our involvement leaves a lot to be desired, and I don't like the feeling of having Myron Streisman peering over my shoulder. It doesn't help to have to face local resentments, and somehow, this murder lacks *core.*'

Delaval raised his eyebrows. 'I don't understand.'

'Oh well, yes, it is early days and we've only just started, but everything is so . . . *superficial.* I don't get any vibrations of anger or passion or violence—'

'Norman was hammered hard enough over the head, sir.'

'I agree, but he's so . . . how can I explain? He's so faceless so far, and I have an odd feeling that's the way he's going to stay. If he does, we're in trouble.'

'Maybe the flesh will come on the whole thing once we've looked at his work schedules,' Delaval suggested.

'Mmm.' Crow's tone was doubtful. 'I'm not so sure. That cottage, for instance, it was so . . . neat. And it told us nothing. What if Norman's work schedule is the same? Neat, precise, well ordered, and completely non-committal? And I have the feeling that's the way it's going to turn out.'

'So how are we going to play it?' Delaval asked.

The waiter entered the room with a whisky for Crow and a glass of lager for Delaval. Crow waited until the man had left before commenting that he had thought Delaval was a Newcastle Brown man; the northerner discounted the remark.

'You go south, you drink what they drink.'

'Then it should be cider,' Crow argued.

'A chap's got to draw the line. But I was saying—'

'How are we going to play it?' Crow nodded thoughtfully. 'Well, it seems to me we've got to push along certain lines. Whatever our friend Grainger says, we have to look closely at what's been going wrong with the Ottershaw operation. Myron Streisman is convinced that Norman's death is only the external evidence of company problems — I don't go along with that, but maybe there's a germ of truth in it. Certainly, Streisman's own appointments policy sets these people up like a glass menagerie: they're of a kind, to the extent that they seem to have sublimated many of their drives into this job they're doing at Ottershaw. That may, or may not, be significant.'

'With respect, sir, I'm inclined to the latter view.'

'That's as may be,' Crow said, and sipped his whisky, grimaced and added some water to it. 'But we can't afford not to follow the hunches of Myron Streisman, to some little distance, at least.'

'I still think—'

'Let me do *my* thinking out loud first, Delaval,' Crow remonstrated. 'The first line of enquiry is connected with the company. Indeed, at this stage I don't see a second line at all, because there's damn all in the local files that we can seize on.'

'It depends really what you mean by company matters,' Delaval suggested.

'Well, as I see it, we need to check on Norman's later activities in the company, to see what he was getting on with. That means talking to his secretary—'

'A bonny lass. I saw her—'

'*I'll* talk to her,' Crow said firmly. 'And to the other senior people at the site. And I'll check out his notebook with them, as well. Otherwise, there's a couple more things that need checking: namely, the company problems that Fred Norman, to our knowledge, was handling. So, while I chat up this secretary you obviously noticed at the site, you'll be pursuing other lines of enquiry.'

Delaval frowned into his lager. 'Such as?'

Crow managed to keep his face straight. 'I seem to recall that when we worked together in Newcastle you had a certain . . . *entry* to the homes of the gentry, merely because of your name.'

Delaval assumed a weary expression. 'But I've already explained—'

'I think you're going to have to explain again,' Crow said, and allowed the glimmer of a smile to touch his lugubrious mouth. 'Of the two of us, it seems to me you're tailor-made to have a word with Brigadier Leveson. Tomorrow.'

'And what will you be doing, sir? In case I need to contact you?'

'I'm going back to Ottershaw,' Crow explained. 'With the notebook, and with the intention of pressing a few people a little harder.'

* * *

The Chief Constable's cooperation certainly extended next morning to the swift provision of a police car and driver for Crow when he made the request of the car pool to be driven to the Ottershaw plant. He was able to test more easily this time the security arrangements that Grainger had mentioned: while Grainger's car had not been stopped, Crow's certainly was, and only when he had explained his business was he allowed to proceed on to the site. Through the back window he noted, nevertheless, that other vehicles entering behind him were not stopped, presumably because their drivers, or the vehicles themselves, were known to the man at the site entrance. He had to agree, silently, with Grainger's early assessment of the situation: it would not have been difficult for a workman on this site to get to know it well; equally, while the perimeter could become familiar to outsiders, it was unlikely that they could have really obtained the kind of detailed information that would have prevented them stumbling about in the dark in such a way as to attract attention.

It was a point worth considering and holding.

Crow was directed towards the workshop and laboratory section of the site when he asked to see Ray Grainger. He discovered that the hut buildings in that area in fact were also used as offices; he could hear the clattering of typewriters in a typing pool, and some of the names on the doors he passed were already familiar to him. The title of *Board Room* was too dignified for the long, sparsely furnished room into which he was finally ushered, however: the table gleamed, and the chairs were comfortable, with embossed folders and brochures scattered about the side tables, and maps of the site adorning the walls, but it all bore an air of solid activity rather than executive comfort, and Ray Grainger looked different too, rising from his seat tieless and shirt-sleeved.

'I'm sorry,' Crow apologized. 'I hope you're not deeply involved . . . I mean, if I'm breaking something up—'

Grainger shook his head vehemently. 'No, not at all. Come in, Superintendent. We've been at this since seven-thirty, more or less, and we're due a break.' He pressed the buzzer on his desk and spoke into the intercom. 'Janet, bring us in some coffee, now, will you? And for our guest.'

The other men in the room were staring at Crow with barely concealed interest. That they knew who he was, he had no doubt; that they had been warned about his skeletal appearance, he also had no doubt; their surprise was still somewhat amusing, though his amusement was tinged with a vague irritation. Some people managed to mask their surprise when they saw his bald, domed skull and deep-set eyes, but this group were as one in their frank appraisal. Perhaps Myron Streisman men *were* of a type.

'You won't have met my colleagues,' Grainger was saying smoothly, 'so I'd better make the introductions. This is Pete Harris, the Exploration Manager.'

The young man with the fleshy face, pugnacious jaw and dark hair held out his hand. Crow shook it; Harris's grip was strong and competitive: a man of commitment, and with the impetuosity of the young in a position of responsibility. Crow turned away as he was introduced next to Ted Nicholas, the mineralogist, a faded, middle-aged man with vague eyes and round shoulders, but he was aware of Pete Harris moving to one side, still staring at him as though making judgments, weighing him in the balance.

'And this is John Wood, the Senior Metallurgist,' Grainger was continuing, drawing forward a tall, bespectacled man with a reddish-coloured beard and pouched, tired eyes. 'Together, apart from O'Connor, who's recently joined us to take Fred Norman's place, we comprise the senior planning team on the Ottershaw project. O'Connor's not here at the moment, by the way, because he's got a fair bit of field work to do — sort of get to grips with things as a new man. You'll be able to meet him later; he's with Alan Fairfield, the Transport Manager at the moment. Ah . . . and this is Janet, with the coffee.'

The group snickered dutifully and accepted cups of coffee as the small woman in the brown dress handed them out from the tray she had carried in. Crow smiled as she offered him a cup; her eyes flickered up to him, nervously, but she did not return the smile. Instead, she glanced quickly towards Grainger.

'That'll be all, Janet, except that if Mr O'Connor comes in, send him straight in, will you?'

The small group sat around the table sipping their coffee, and a short, awkward silence fell. Crow was disinclined to break it; instead, he gave every appearance of merely enjoying his coffee, and he let Grainger sweat it out.

At last Ray Grainger cleared his throat and rattled his cup in its saucer. 'Well, Superintendent, are there any . . . ah . . . developments in the case?'

Crow smiled. 'Things are always developing, Mr Grainger. The trouble is, usually not fast enough, or clearly enough. That's why I'm here, really. To fill in a few bits and pieces.'

Pete Harris leaned forward, his jaw jutting. 'I'm not sure that there's very much we can do to help you.'

'None of us really knew Fred very well outside work,' John Wood offered, stroking his reddish beard nervously.

'But you had plenty of contact with him at work,' Crow said.

Nevertheless, as he talked with them for the next few minutes it became apparent that even on the site the contact they had had with the murdered Environmental Coordinator could not have been described as intimate. Wood agreed that he had worked on metallurgical matters with Fred Norman, but only intermittently. And Ted Nicholas had helped him in the setting up of the testing gauges for quantifying the existing levels of dust deposition. 'We were trying to acquire a range of meteorological parameters, in order that, when mining *did* begin, we could measure the deposits formerly experienced against those likely to arise.' But he too denied that their work together had been anything other than rare and lacking in opportunity to produce relationships which might have provided John Crow with information about the dead man.

But this experience was nothing new to John Crow. A man died a violent death and his friends began to fade away, his acquaintances suddenly hadn't known him, and his colleagues confessed only to having seen him as part of the background to their working lives, never a real, physical, living part of it. Death could do that to a group of people: they wanted no involvement. They had witnessed nothing; they knew nothing. The problem was, one could never be certain whether they were in fact telling the truth. In this case it could well be that they were. Fred Norman could have been the self-effacing kind of individual whose most positive action had been to get murdered.

'And what about you, Mr Harris?' Crow asked, turning to the Exploration Manager. 'How well did you know Mr Norman? Did you spend much time working with him?'

Harris stared at his coffee for a moment without replying. He had a soft mouth, a spoiled child's mouth, with all the aggression that could suddenly transform its shape and weakness into anger. And when he looked up at Crow his eyes held flint-coloured points of light that seemed to move and change, points of watchfulness. 'I suppose you could say I worked with Fred more than anyone else in this room,' he said.

'That would be inevitable,' Ray Grainger murmured.

'Inevitable?' Crow queried.

Pete Harris nodded. 'The baseline studies that Fred instituted for the feasibility study, they involved hydrological studies — we were trying to work out chemical parameters in the streams — terrestrial and ecological studies. It was inevitable that he would work fairly closely with me, because it was the impact of the mining and exploration work upon the atmosphere, the ecology, the water supplies, the local communities and their resources, that the study was all about. So, yes, we spent a fair bit of time together on several projects.'

'You'll have got to know him well, then.'

'As well as any here.' The flinty points were changing, moving in his eyes. 'But that's not saying very much.'

'How do you mean?'

'The others here have already said it, in a different way. Fred was pretty much a loner. He didn't seek our company; he didn't need it. He did his work well, but then shot off to his cottage and we saw little of him. I met him for an occasional beer, when we were out on moor locations — lunchtime drink in a local village pub, that sort of thing. But he never said very much. A widower, and pretty close. That was it.'

The picture Crow had already been building up was merely receiving confirmation. He tried another tack. 'I wonder if you'll be able to tell me what his work schedule was during the last few weeks before his death?'

Harris tugged at his lip with a doubtful finger. 'I hadn't seen too much of him these last few weeks. But—'

'It was Janet who had worked as his secretary,' Ray Grainger interrupted. 'She'll be able to give you that sort of detail.'

Something made John Crow turn back to Harris, nevertheless. The Exploration Manager was staring at him hesitantly, the tip of his tongue touching his upper lip. Crow felt the young man wanted to say something but was not certain this was the right time. After a few moments silence Crow nodded. 'All right, I'll have a word with her shortly. Meanwhile . . . I've been up to Norman's cottage. I found a notebook there. It had a few scribbles in it which mean nothing to me, but perhaps you could help.'

John Crow handed the notebook to Pete Harris. He did not want to take it. He stared at it for a long moment, and there was reluctance in the manner in which he finally took the book. He skipped quickly through the pages, and shook his head. 'Nothing important, as far as I can see.' He went to hand it back, but Crow gestured towards the others. Ray Grainger took it, and riffled through it as Wood and Nicholas looked over his shoulder. Grainger frowned.

'Just notes, as Pete says. As far as these comments on the rock are concerned—'

'They're wrong,' Ted Nicholas interrupted. His glance became even vaguer as he frowned, thinking back. 'The rock in this area — it's locally known as killas, metamorphosed sediments really — comprises thermally metamorphosed Devonian silts tone, mudstone and altered basic volcanics. It holds three major vein sets and all the veins carry wolframite. But the gradings he's noted are erroneous: they are of too low a concentrate.'

Crow stared at the mineralogist. 'Are these errors of any importance?'

The vague eyes became puzzled. 'Importance? None at all. We're merely carrying out feasibility studies. We don't have an operational plant yet. We've taken extracts provided by the consultant engineers—'

'I explained,' Grainger interrupted. 'Craydon Engineering are sub-contractors of ours.'

'—and we've made certain calculations on the basis of their core samples. But important? Not at all.'

'Why would he note such errors in this book?' Crow asked. Nicholas shrugged his round shoulders and turned away dismissively. 'Maybe he wouldn't have realized the errors. He wasn't a qualified mineralogist.'

Grainger was looking at the table that Norman had drawn in the notebook. 'I don't know why he's got this here.'

'What does it mean?' Crow asked.

Grainger showed him the notebook. 'It's just a summary of the drilling we've done recently at the site. These capital letters — they'll relate to the phases. Phase A was pre-Streisman. I can tell you about 30 holes were drilled by percussion methods. These phases are what we've done. Phase Band C, we drilled 18 holes by percussion and reverse circulation. Phase D and E, 17 holes by percussion and diamond drilling.'

'And the figures in the right hand column?'

Grainger shrugged. 'Depth of the drilling, in metres. Nothing odd about the information. No secrets there.'

'You don't know why he should note it?' Crow asked.

Grainger looked around at his colleagues and shook his head. 'Can't imagine. The information is accessible to any of us, just by asking the Craydon Engineering people. They keep the charts; they do the drilling for us. I reckon this was just for his own information. It's . . . meaningless, in terms of practical use. To him, I mean, personally. He'd only have to ask, if he needed it for publicity . . . though that probably *was* the reason. He'll have needed it for some environmental meeting or other. With Brigadier Leveson, maybe.'

'So the notebook entries have little significance.'

'*I* would have said, none,' Pete Harris suggested. But the note of aggression in his voice held something else buried under the pugnacity. Crow could not define it, but he noted it. He smiled, and aware of Harris's eyes fixed on him, he looked again at the notebook, thoughtfully, before returning it to his pocket. 'Ah, well, it was just possible it would be of some use, but if you gentlemen assure me . . . I'll take up no more of your time, Mr Grainger. Janet, you said, was his secretary?'

* * *

She was nervous and fluttery and scared that she should be interviewed by a member of the Murder Squad, and when he asked her what Fred Norman had been like she began to cry gently. He had been a *nice* man, she explained; considerate, quiet, polite, with her. He spent little time with the others, but once or twice he had given her a lift to Ottershaw when she had missed the service bus, and he had talked to her a little of his life in America when his wife had been alive. It had been a bitter blow, the loss of his wife: he had withdrawn, toyed with religion for a while but not seriously, and then finally had found his salvation in his work.

'He worked ever so hard, Superintendent Crow. Took papers home with him all the time, and never seemed to begrudge the time he spent. And he *believed* in what he was doing too. He did get upset recently, of course, over the way he felt Brigadier Leveson had treated him, but that was because he had done so much work on the matter, and he felt the Brigadier had let him down, not been straight with him, you know what I mean?'

But she hadn't known what he was doing, particularly of late. She had kept his diary, but it produced little information: meetings in Ottershaw; a few visits to Brigadier Leveson; a trip to Exeter; a tour of the garages that serviced Streisman vehicles. He had been busy on something, though, she was sure. A report of some kind. But *she* hadn't typed it, and if the Superintendent could give her a little while to think, she could probably work it out, remember who the report had been for . . . Just at this moment, she couldn't recall, but there had been something he had said . . .

* * *

A cold wind had risen, and there was a hint of rain in the air, with hazy mists darkening the line of Dartmoor, and drifting towards the pale china-clay tips scarring the slopes above Lee Moor. The sky was a mackerel colour, patchy with dark cloud, and Crow turned up the collar of his coat as he walked out towards the solid-waste disposal area, where he had been told he would find Alan Fairfield, the man in charge of Streisman transport. O'Connor, the dead man's replacement, was with him, apparently, and Crow walked among the curious glances of the yellow-jacketed, red-helmeted workmen on the site with the thought that though safety might demand it, he was determined not to perch one of those red helmets on his own domed skull.

He found the two men he sought standing near the weather station that had been set up beside the solid-waste disposal area. After he had introduced himself, Crow found his curious glance at the weather station led to an explanation from O'Connor regarding the sophisticated complex of automatic recording instruments, placed on the specially laid turf and measuring wind speed, rainfall, temperature and the amount of pollution in the atmosphere. 'It's one of our main concerns, of course, and the layout that Fred Norman established is a pretty good one.'

'It's Fred Norman I came over to have a talk about,' Crow said gently.

O'Connor, a thin, prematurely bald man with bright blue eyes, shrugged. 'Well, there's nothing I can tell you about him at all. I didn't know him; we never met.'

'Have you taken over his work schedules?'

'To some extent. And I have all his working papers. Janet can let you see them if you want them. But beyond that—'

'What was he working on recently, do you know?' Crow asked.

O'Connor took out a pipe, tapped it against the heel of his hand, and, frowning, sucked at it thoughtfully. He shook his head. 'Nothing in particular. Routine, as far as I can see. Certainly he's left no major ends untied for me. Sorry I can't help you more . . . If there's any way I *can* help, I'd be pleased . . . but I really don't see . . .'

Fred Norman's successor was in no hurry to get deeply involved with the investigation into his predecessor's murder. After a few more brief questions that elicited nothing of value, Crow allowed the new Environmental Manager to hurry away.

'It's understandable,' Alan Fairfield said with a wry smile.

Crow turned to him. Fairfield was a short, thickset man with wiry, crinkly hair, sandy in colour and thick at the nape of his neck. His eyebrows were heavy, his nose strong, and there was strength in his mouth too, thin-lipped and determined. As Transport Manager he would have to handle a notoriously wild group of men, the lorry drivers, and he would need to be tough, and in his eyes there was a hint of a wildness that he had not left behind either.

'Why understandable?' Crow asked.

Fairfield shrugged his broad shoulders in the leather jacket he wore. 'It's bad enough for the rest of us, being questioned. For O'Connor, well, he's stepped into a new job and an important one, flown in from Germany to do it, and there's no way he would want to be bogged down by enquiries such as yours. He's got his own job to handle, and it's big enough without complications.'

'Do you have much to do with the environmental side of things, then?'

Fairfield stared at Crow for a moment, his eyes narrowing thoughtfully. Then he jerked his head. 'Come on over to my office — we can talk there, over a cup of coffee.'

He led the way, hunched in his jacket, picking his way past the only area of mud that seemed to be present on what was, Crow felt, a remarkably clean site for a mining operation, until they reached a single-storey building located near the old workings.

'Easier to keep the office near the main gates,' the Transport Manager explained as he paused in the entrance to the building. 'Keep an eye on the cowboys then, as well as our own people.'

'Cowboys?'

'The lads who drive for our sub-contractors. There's maybe thirty or so of them who come on the site from time to time, and they can cause problems. But, well, they're all right.' He grinned suddenly, displaying a gap-toothed smile. 'I sorted one out last year and bust a knuckle doing it, but everything's OK as a result.'

'Here on the site?' Crow asked.

'No, no — hell, if Streisman heard I'd brawled on site there'd be hell to pay. No, it was down in Ottershaw — at the Miner's Arms. I'd had a few drinks and so had he, and there was an argument. We settled it in the yard at the back. Still see him from time to time here. No hard feelings.'

The office was little more than a cabin, but it was warm, and the lad in the outer room quickly brought in two mugs of steaming coffee, so that by the time Crow had been given a chair and Fairfield had divested himself of helmet and jacket the atmosphere was pleasant and comfortable.

'Well, then . . . Superintendent, is it?' Fairfield raised his heavy eyebrows. 'What can I do for you?'

'Well, as I was asking—'

'Ah, the environmental involvement, yes.' Fairfield sipped noisily at his coffee. 'We all have *some* involvement with that — I mean, the feasibility study largely depends on what Fred Norman would be coming up with. If the scheme just isn't on environmentally, a lot of money goes down the drain. So, as I said, we're all involved.'

'And your particular involvement?'

Fairfield's hands were broad, his fingers stubby and powerful. He clenched them around his coffee mug. 'Obvious, really. Fumes from the lorries is one thing, on and off the site; another is, I need to monitor the transport arrangements generally, and that means access roads to the site. But I had to work with Fred Norman on that to ensure that the access roads we planned didn't interfere in any way with the community — or awkward customers like Brigadier Leveson.'

'His name seems to be cropping up all over the place,' Crow remarked quietly.

'He's one of our biggest headaches,' Fairfield said, glowering, 'and he causes me problems, I can tell you. But that's another matter — though Fred was involved with that, too. You'd best see Leveson about that one, though, and not get a garbled version second-hand from me.'

'Hmmm.' Crow hesitated. 'I gather that you saw rather more of Fred Norman recently than the others.'

'I did?' Fairfield seemed surprised. 'I don't know if that was the case. Off site I rarely saw him at all: he was a loner.'

'But on site, recently, you'd been working fairly closely, I understand. Or so Ray Grainger informs me.'

Fairfield stared at Crow; there was a certain uneasiness in his eyes, and after a few moments he turned his head to stare out of the window to the grey skies. 'Did Ray tell you what Norman was working with me about?'

'No.'

Fairfield looked back to Crow; whatever unease had lurked in his eyes was gone now, but his glance was still watchful. 'You've heard about the trouble with lorries at Ottershaw, though?'

'I've experienced some of it.'

'Who hasn't?' Fairfield scowled. 'It's a real headache, and me and Fred Norman, we were the ones in the firing line. I still am, for that matter. You see, lorries have been trundling through the village for years, to and from the clay pits. But opening up this site meant an increase in traffic. We thought we'd got it sorted out as a problem — and then Leveson sold us down the river. We're still haggling about it, but meanwhile the lorries still have to come through the village to get to this site.'

'Fred Norman acted as the public relations man in this problem?' Crow asked.

'You could say that — though he was also involved in all the planning implications and the negotiations with Leveson. My involvement with Fred concerned the village, largely.'

'And this is what you were working with him on, just before he died?' Crow asked.

Fairfield was silent for a short while. He sipped at his coffee, thinking, seemingly reluctant to say more, and yet knowing more was expected of him. At last he sighed, and put down his mug. 'I don't know how much you know about the problem at Ottershaw.'

'Only what I've seen — which was a fairly mild sort of protest action, it seemed to me — and what you've told me,' Crow replied. 'What more is there?'

Fairfield cleared his throat noisily. 'Damn sight more. Things have been quiet in fact, since Fred Norman died. It's kind of like they've been scared off a bit; but it'll come up again and the demonstrations will get rougher, if Jack Prince has anything to do with it.'

'Prince?'

Fairfield's mouth moved unpleasantly. 'You'll get to meet him soon enough, I've no doubt. He used to be a shop steward over at Lewforth before he left them — never knew why, but the whisper is there was some money trouble, and he's a shifty bastard all right. I'd guess he's in the Ottershaw thing as much for what he can get — and is getting — out of it for himself.'

'You'd better explain in rather more detail, Mr Fairfield. Demonstrations, you said. Are they with the objective of keeping Streisman vehicles out of Ottershaw?'

'Streisman — and others, too. Ever since the a — the accident.'

'Someone was hurt?' Crow asked.

'Killed,' Fairfield said, and stared down at his coffee.

'One of your lorries?' Crow queried softly.

Fairfield stood up violently and shook his head. 'Damn it, no, it wasn't one of our lorries. That was what Fred Norman came to see me about, and worked with me over the lorry schedules a few months back. Look, this is the way it was. This kid . . . this girl . . . she was in the main street after dark and she got knocked down, a hit-and-run driver, and she was killed. It caused a hell of a storm, you can imagine; the police were called in, and they came out to see me as well as the people at Lewforth, but our vehicles got a clean bill of health, not only from our mileage and work records, but also from vehicle inspections — as you'd know, a check on vehicle damage would have shown if any of our lorries had been responsible. No, we were clean, and so were the Lewforth people.'

'The driver hasn't been found?'

'Neither driver nor vehicle.' Fairfield shook his head angrily. 'But bloody Jack Prince won't let go of it. He's been whipping things up in Ottershaw and in the county — and beyond, too, so I hear. And Marlene Park is right with him, tears and all — you can imagine the impact that has!'

'Marlene Park?'

'The dead girl's mother.'

Crow stared at him coolly. 'I would have thought the sympathy she would have aroused—'

'Sympathy?' Fairfield rounded on Crow with a surprising anger in his tone. 'Now look, don't waste too much sympathy on *that* whore. She's shouting loud just because she can see money in it, and because Jack Prince is pushing her — and maybe for other reasons too.'

'Such as?'

'Guilt, maybe.' Fairfield stopped suddenly, as though he wished he had not said what he did. Crow waited, and reluctantly the Transport Manager went on. 'Anyway, they've been putting pressure on, there were demonstrations in the main street, they closed it best part of a week, and it was then that Fred came back to me and did a complete check again. But all our drivers were accounted for; all our vehicles clean. Fred was satisfied. Jack Prince wasn't.'

'How do you mean?'

'I wasn't there, so this is just hearsay, but I gather that Fred paid one of his rare visits to the Miner's Arms and met Jack Prince there. They had words. I don't know more than that. And I'm certainly not saying that Prince had anything to do with Fred Norman's death. But . . .'

Crow let the word hang in the air for a little while. He finished his coffee, and Fairfield resumed his seat, shaking his head. At last, Crow said, 'You made some remark about Mrs Park being little better than a whore.'

'Fact.' Fairfield snarled unpleasantly. 'Not gossip. She was divorced, by all accounts, seven or eight years ago. Her daughter would've been about seven at the time, I suppose. She's been with some bloke or another ever since — the occasional Lewforth man, the odd driver, strangely enough, but most recently our friend Jack Prince. She's been sleeping with that bastard for a year or more, though I suspect he'd have been replaced long before now if it hadn't been for the death of the kid.'

Something was flaring angrily in Fairfield's eyes, and Crow watched him silently for a little while. 'Do you have any children, Mr Fairfield?'

Alan Fairfield shot a quick glance in Crow's direction, then shook his head. There was an odd sneer in his tone when he replied. 'My wife doesn't want children. She doesn't want much of me either, for that matter. She wants what I send her — she's up at Leominster — but that satisfies her. No, no children. Why do you ask?'

'You seem . . . particularly angry . . . bitter about the death of this girl . . .'

'Freda Park.' Fairfield shrugged. 'No, it's not that—'

'And you mentioned that Marlene Park might have feelings of guilt.'

Fairfield was silent again for a little while. He drained his mug of the now almost cold coffee and pushed it away from him. 'The talk is . . . the talk is that bloody Marlene Park and Jack Prince were where they always were that night. Down at the Miner's Arms. Half-cut, both of them, and just waiting for closing time to stagger off to bed. The girl, meanwhile — and she was fifteen, mind — was out in the street instead of being at home. Out in the street at ten at night, going up to the pub maybe, no one seems to know. And it was then that some — some clown came down that road and hit her. Killed her.' He looked up at Crow, an inexplicable ferocity in his eyes. 'It need never have happened, Superintendent. If that woman hadn't been drinking with Jack Prince, the girl maybe wouldn't have been out in the street. And she'd never have been . . . knocked down and killed.'

'And you think maybe the mother now has feelings of guilt, which push her into this campaign against lorries in Ottershaw?'

'Well, if she hasn't, she bloody well ought to have!' Fairfield glared at Crow angrily. 'If she hadn't been in that pub the girl wouldn't have died, this campaign wouldn't have had its major impetus, and we wouldn't be getting the hassle we are!'

A curious kind of anger, Crow thought as he walked back to the car waiting for him; an anger that was somehow rooted in odd logic, and based on unstructured premises. It was as though Alan Fairfield blamed the events in Ottershaw for the death of Fred Norman — or was it merely that he resented the interference he was suffering as a result of the death of the girl? Crow felt confused, disorientated suddenly. A thread had been snapped in his mind, somewhere; he had lost direction.

He hoped Delaval was having better luck with his interview.

* * *

Devon wasn't like Northumberland. The hills were smaller, rounder, softer, lacking the harsh sweep of the northern ones, even on Dartmoor itself. The red earth banks of the rivers hadn't the black rocks of the Northumberland streams, and the air was too languid, too lulling for a head accustomed to the cold bracing winds of the north. Pretty, oh, it was pretty enough, with its combes and valleys and streams and tors, but for the first time Delaval found himself missing the wild coastline and booming seas and windswept heathered hills that he had known since childhood and so recently left. Somehow this all seemed so small to him after Northumberland.

Not that the Leveson estate was small.

The entrance lay through a gateway flanked by stone lions on pedestals; lichen-covered, they snarled silently with discoloured fangs as Delaval drove past their sightless eyes. The carriageway looped through a belt of trees before dipping down to a deer park beside which a small, bright stream meandered, and on a rise, at the far end of the carriageway, fronted by rhododendrons, formal gardens and wide stone steps, stood Cartmel Grange, the home of Brigadier Leveson and, apparently, of generations of his family before him. When Delaval parked near the steps, on the gravelled space provided, he could look back over a lush valley towards a tree-lined hill beyond which, if his memory of the map served him correctly, the plans for a roadway to the Ottershaw plant would lay an access track for the lorries bypassing the village. Nor would it make much difference to the valley, it seemed to him. It would not be visible, and the deer park and meadows that lay below him would be unscarred and unaffected.

Brigadier Leveson had left instructions that he would meet Inspector Delaval in the library, which proved to be a high-ceilinged, high-windowed room whose walls were lined with volumes in elegant bindings. On inspection, Delaval realized that most of the books were of some vintage: he could discover little that had been published within the last thirty years, so he suspected that neither the Brigadier nor his predecessor had regarded reading as a worthwhile pastime. Unless they were satisfied with Edwardian and Victorian volumes.

The Brigadier himself, when he entered the library, gave Delaval every satisfaction, for he was all that the policeman had imagined he would be. He was six feet in height, with a ramrod back and a lean, spare frame. He was in his mid-fifties, so must have enjoyed a swift rise through the ranks to have been able to retire so early, for Delaval gathered the Brigadier had been at Cartmel Grange, in retirement, for at least five years. His features were hawkish, his nose sharply inquisitive, his eyes close-set, and his mouth thinly uncompromising. He did not walk, he strode, and when he faced Delaval it was with his back to the fireplace, a classical position with his hands locked behind his back. Delaval had pictured a caricature and had got one — but caricature or not, this man, he felt as he met Leveson's cold glance, could be ruthless, committed and even dangerous.'

'Delaval,' the Brigadier said thoughtfully. 'From the north country?'

That's right, sir. But—'

'Not related to—'

'No, sir,' Delaval interrupted firmly. Even in the Newcastle area he was asked the question, and he was tired of explaining that if he was in any way related to the landed gentry of Northumberland it was probably from the wrong side of the blanket. The terraces of Byker had been his nurturing ground, not the halls of Northumberland, but he had not expected to have to answer yet again, here in Devon. At least it showed that Leveson was no different from other landed gentry: a closed society in many ways, inward-looking, always searching for their own kind. Perhaps they were uneasy in the modern, thrusting world, as they saw their values eroded; perhaps it was why the Brigadier was so committed to upsetting the plans of the Streisman company, and was proving so difficult to deal with.

The Brigadier was rocking slightly on his heels as he stared at Delaval. 'All right, then, young man, what is it you want to see me about?'

'We're making enquiries into the murder of a man called Norman, the Environmental Coordinator at the Ottershaw project.'

'Can't help you. Made that clear to the local police. I suggest you talk to them.'

'It isn't the way things work, sir,' Delaval said firmly. 'We've taken the matter over now, and will have to pursue the enquiries we deem necessary.'

'Deem?' The Brigadier gave a short, barking laugh that held no amusement. 'For a moment you sounded more like a lawyer than a policeman.'

'I took a law degree, sir, at Newcastle.'

Leveson's cold eyes regarded him with a glint of interest. 'Is that so? Well, I'll tell you, Delaval, I've just about had my fill of lawyers of recent years.'

'Yes, sir?'

The Brigadier strode across to the tall windows and stared out over the deer park, hands still locked behind his back. 'They tell you one thing, offer you advice, and then, damn me, when the other side comes up with an argument they back down! I'm not prepared to do that, Delaval, I'm not prepared to back down on anything when I know I'm right.'

And he was the kind of man, Delaval considered, who would always regard himself as right. Aloud, he said, 'Was it a legal dispute you were having with Fred Norman, sir?'

The Brigadier's back stiffened, but he did not turn around. 'Where do you get the information that I had a dispute with . . . Norman?'

'I think it's fairly common knowledge, Brigadier.'

'*Common* knowledge, is it?' The Brigadier snorted in contemptuous derision. 'I don't give a damn what the *common* knowledge is! I was in no dispute with Norman — though I'll admit I was angered by his — his recalcitrance and his lack of faith. My dispute is with the Streisman Corporation — and that's not the same thing as saying it was with their Environmental Coordinator!'

'Perhaps you'd like to tell me about it, sir.'

Brigadier Leveson turned and glared at Delaval. He walked back to the fireplace and resumed his previous position. He looked around the room as though reassuring himself of his possessions and his position, and he said harshly, 'I'm not certain it's any of your business. It has nothing to do with the death of the man.'

'With respect, Brigadier, any murder investigation consists of a large number of facts, many of them irrelevant, many of them useless — but until we know all the facts that surround the central situation we can't be certain we've built up the total picture — and without the total picture, a bad mistake might be made.'

'I see that,' Leveson admitted grudgingly, 'but my dispute with Streisman—'

'I think it would be of considerable assistance if you could explain it to me, sir.'

The Brigadier considered the matter at some length.

Finally he nodded and walked across the room to open the mahogany cupboard standing beside the bookshelves. He took out a cut-glass tumbler and poured himself a stiff measure of malt whisky. He glanced vaguely towards Delaval, and then dismissed the thought of offering the policeman a drink. It might have been consideration of Delaval's being on duty; more likely, it was a gesture of contempt. An officer did not drink with other ranks.

'When my uncle died five years ago,' the Brigadier said, 'I inherited the estate, so I retired from the Army and came here to farm. I found the estate in reasonably good order, though there were improvements to be undertaken. My uncle was an old man . . .' He glared at the whisky and rocked on his heels. 'It might have been his age that caused him to enter into certain unwise contractual arrangements.'

'With the Streisman Corporation?' Delaval asked.

'Among others,' the Brigadier answered vaguely. 'But they were certainly not of the kind I would have contemplated — and I am in dispute with the lawyers about them.'

'What kind of dispute?'

The Brigadier took a stiff swallow of whisky, and blinked. 'I don't think I need go into details. Let's just say I consider, whatever the lawyers say, that some of the contracts bound the estate beyond the lifetime of the incumbent — my uncle — in a way that was unreasonable, and bind his successors in an unacceptable way.'

'Is the estate an entailed one, then?' Delaval asked. The Brigadier shot a quick glance in his direction, then shook his head. 'No. But that's not the point. He was an old man, and didn't understand the ways of business . . .'

'What did the Streisman contracts involve?' Delaval asked.

'They were several.' The Brigadier suddenly motioned with his glass and strode back to the window. 'Come here.'

Delaval obeyed the peremptory order and stood beside Leveson, looking down over the deer park and the meadows beyond.

'You see the meadow beyond the deer park? The first agreement reached with Streisman related to rights of way — a roadway which would service the site when it was fully operational. For that, the princely sum of £200,000 was offered, and paid.'

Delaval swallowed. 'That sounds . . . er . . . reasonable.'

Leveson glowered at him. 'If it had related merely to the roadway, yes, but there was more to it than that, as Norman was quick to point out to me two years ago. There were also certain other options written into the agreement, which were hardly to the advantage of the estate.'

'What kind of options?' Delaval asked.

Leveson hesitated for a moment, then turned aside, put down his cut-glass tumbler and walked towards the bureau that stood in the far corner of the library. From a drawer the Brigadier took out a thick, folded sheet and spread it out on the table in the centre of the room. 'If I am to satisfy your curiosity,' he said drily, 'you'd better look at this.'

It was a map of the Leveson estate. The grounds to Cartmel Grange were clearly delineated, but the holdings beyond that were extensive, running the length of the valley and crossing the line of hills to the east of the house. The Brigadier stabbed a nicotine-stained finger on the map.

'The options,' he said harshly, 'were, basically, two. There were others, but they are unimportant. These two were the ones that enraged me, for I consider my uncle was . . . *conned,* I think the word is. You see this marking here? It's the site of old workings that date back to the sixteenth century. They've not been worked for over a hundred years now, and, naturally enough, they have virtually disappeared, merged into the landscape. One of the options available under the contract, however, would be that Streisman should be allowed, having given two years' notice, to open a new mining operation at that site.'

'You mean if they find that the mining of wolframite is commercially viable at Ottershaw, they could take up the option to open this shaft also?' When the Brigadier nodded, Delaval suggested, 'At a price, surely.'

Leveson scowled at the map. 'A further £100,000 would then become payable, in that event. But that's not the point. Can you imagine the impact it would have, mining just here? It would destroy the whole character of the estate!'

Delaval nodded. 'And the second option?'

'The agreement allowed for a road to be run to the west of the hill, just here. The objective, of course, is to make a more direct access to the plant above Ottershaw.'

'And relieve the traffic through the village,' Delaval added. 'But I don't quite see what objections you can have to that. I mean, you wouldn't even be able to see it from here, and it would make little if any difference to the estate lands themselves.'

Brigadier Leveson snorted. 'Your words are an echo of those used by that man Norman, when he came here. Like him, you fail to see the point. It's true that to cut that access road would make little difference to the deer park — and perhaps a more public-spirited man would think of the villagers. But the point is this: what would you, as a lawyer, say to me if I allowed that road to be cut, under the option?'

Delaval shook his head, puzzled. 'I suppose . . . well, it would merely be confirmation of an existing agreement.'

'Exactly,' Leveson said with a note of triumph in his voice. 'And I'd have no leg to stand on if I then argued against the taking up of the *mining* option, would I? No court would accept that I should allow one option to be taken up while denying the existence of the other. So, I'm refusing to allow that road to be cut, and to hell with them.'

'But surely severance of the unreasonable terms could have been negotiated with Streisman,' Delaval suggested.

Leveson snorted again and reached for his whisky tumbler. He drained it of the golden liquid, and then walked across to pour himself another stiff drink. He shook his head. 'Let's just say negotiations broke down. But all this is beside the point. It's got nothing to do with Norman's death. Indeed, there's no way in which I can help you.'

Delaval was not so sure. He stared at the map. 'You said Norman came to see you.'

'That's right.'

'When was that?'

'Months ago.'

'The last time . . . was when?' Delaval asked.

There was a slight hesitation before the Brigadier replied. 'It would be about . . . maybe six, eight weeks ago.'

'What offer did Norman make?'

'He'd already made the offer, earlier. This visit . . . it was . . .' Leveson hesitated again, glowering at his glass. His hand was clenched around it, the knuckles standing out whitely. Delaval guessed the interview with Norman had been a stormy one. 'The visit,' Leveson said finally, in a grinding voice, 'was to tell me that Myron Streisman would not approve the terms. I was to be held to my uncle's contract. At least, that was to be the effect of the company actions.'

'I don't quite understand,' Delaval said.

Brigadier Leveson looked at him with anger in his close-set eyes. 'Then I shall explain to you the methods of big business, and American corporations in particular. The offer that Norman came to me with months ago was simple: if I did not oppose the road and the other option, but in particular the road — for the company is faced with problems at the village — they would reach a financial agreement with me.'

'Compensate you?'

'Not in a straight manner. Look again at the map.' Leveson did not approach the table, but stood whisky glass in hand as Delaval looked at the map. 'You see how my estates abut almost on the Ottershaw pilot site?'

Delaval nodded. 'Very close.'

'What do you know about open-cast mining systems, Inspector?'

'Very little, really.'

Brigadier Leveson smiled thinly. 'Well, there's a certain inevitability about them. As they progress, they demand more land, of course. Now, what my friend Norman had proposed was that as the land was taken up and encroachments became necessary on that tongue of land which belongs to me, I would be paid a royalty — one and a half per cent, no less, on all wolframite mined on that tongue . . . *That* was to be the price of my failure to oppose the options.'

'They really must have wanted that road west of the hill.'

'They still do. But in my view the agreement would not have been a fair one.'

'So what did Norman come to tell you on his last visit?' Brigadier Leveson stalked towards the table on stiff legs. He plucked a pen from a stand on the table and leaned over the map.

'Norman didn't come of his own volition. I *summoned* him. Certain information had come to my ears, and I taxed him with it. He was unable to deny the truth of what I had heard. And when I upbraided him, he lost his temper — he suggested I was trying to blackmail the company. I did not see it that way. They were buying me off with this new royalty agreement — but it was an agreement they had no intention of honouring.'

'How do you mean?'

Brigadier Leveson began to make thick, swift strokes of the pen on the map. 'I heard that certain land purchases had been made west of the site. I made other enquiries and soon got the drift of things. Oh yes, Streisman would enter into a royalty agreement with me — but then his mining operations would run like *this.*'

Delaval stared at the marks made on the map by the Brigadier.

Bitterly, the Brigadier said, 'Simple, isn't it? You see how it works? That western edge of the mining operation is elongated and moving away from the land which I hold. Deliberately! They will now mine only on their own land, recently purchased! In other words, the new agreement would have been worthless. I would have given up my opposition to the roadway in return for "compensation" that would never have become payable!'

Delaval understood the point the Brigadier was making. He also recalled something he had heard regarding Myron Streisman's business practices. This operation smacked of sharp practice — and yet Streisman's Mormon background was supposed to prevent him from descending to business deals of this kind. But maybe Streisman had reasoned he was only doing what Leveson was trying to do with him. Agreements regarding the options existed, but Leveson did not wish to be bound by them.

'Do you have a court action pending on the options?' Delaval asked.

'I do,' the Brigadier said triumphantly. 'And a planning enquiry too! They'll find they can't ride roughshod over me!'

Delaval stared at him. The picture was clearing. The Streisman operation was hitting difficulties in Ottershaw village: they would be exacerbated by Leveson's actions. And Streisman *would* see this as blackmail by the Brigadier. His answer had been to try to outmanoeuvre Leveson over the royalties offer.

And Fred Norman had had to bear the brunt of the discussion with Leveson.

'When Norman came to see you, did you have . . . words with him?' Delaval asked quietly.

'On which occ . . .' The remark was dragged back; Leveson's eyes were suddenly shadowed with doubt and uncertainty. 'Words?' he asked dully, as though giving his disturbed wits time to reorganize themselves.

'Was there a quarrel?' Delaval persisted.

Leveson had regained control. 'Yes, there was a quarrel. I told Norman what I thought of him, when it became apparent that either he had lied to me or else he did not have the confidence of his employer. But let's be clear about one thing. A quarrel of that kind, it isn't likely to lead to a man's death. After all,' he added viciously, 'I had no need to do any more than I am doing. After all, I'm winning, aren't I?'

Reluctantly Delaval was forced to agree. 'And that was the last time you saw Norman?'

Brigadier Leveson finished his whisky in one gulp and turned towards the door. 'That was. And now you must excuse me. I don't believe there's any other way in which I can help you.'

* * *

'And do you think there is?' John Crow asked Delaval that evening, over dinner.

Delaval wasn't certain. Something about Brigadier Leveson did not ring true. He was left with the feeling that the retired army man had not told him everything he could have done: there was an element of artificiality in his account of the events leading up to a quarrel. He found it difficult to believe that the Brigadier *would* have quarrelled with Norman over the prospect of a hollow agreement; certainly not when he was still holding the whip-hand by delaying the building of the access road through court proceedings and planning enquiries. He sipped the glass of Medoc which the Superintendent had thoughtfully provided with their meal.

'I consider that Brigadier Leveson's activities still require some looking into,' he suggested. 'I'd like to do a bit more burrowing.'

John Crow nodded. 'You do that. Me, I'll follow up another lead entirely, though it's not unconnected with the gallant Brigadier.'

'The road through the village?'

'That. And a gentleman called Jack Prince.'

CHAPTER 3

The Miner's Arms, testifying by its name to a long local involvement with the industry, was located at the far end of Ottershaw village where the road widened before sweeping into the rise of the hill. A gravel car park to the left of the inn provided room for perhaps twenty cars, though the scars on the grass that sloped down to the tiny stream at the back of the building showed that customers were not averse to chancing their skills at negotiating the river bank when fortified by alcohol. The inn itself was an old grey-stoned building that pre-dated much of the village; ivy smothered the front of the structure, all but blanking out two of the windows, and the timbers of the tiny porch that protected the main entrance were weather-beaten and dark-stained.

John Crow stood in the street, looking at the inn. He had left the car at the other end of the village while he walked through the bustle of the mid-morning traffic to appreciate at first hand the problems afflicting the village. There had been no minor incident such as the one he had already witnessed, but he could understand local reaction to belching fumes and the roar of heavy lorries in the main street. In some sections of the street the pavements were narrow, so congested as to force their users to maintain a wary eye for the vehicles that threatened their passage. If the pilot plant proved successful up on the moor, and if Brigadier Leveson was equally successful in preventing the building of the other access road, the village would certainly be faced with a major problem.

Crow had already visited the terrace house where Marlene Park lived. It was one of a modest, grey-slated group whose blank faces stared out over the village itself from the vantage point of a steep, winding hill. The sun had been shining when Crow climbed the hill, and the ascent had taken the breath from his chest: he felt he was getting old. The pause while he had knocked, without answer, on Marlene Park's door, had allowed him to recover, and enjoy the view of the village. It had also given him time to think about the girl who had been killed. She would have left this house and walked down the hill in the darkness, perhaps to meet her mother and her mother's reputed lover at the public house. The vehicle that killed her would have come sweeping round that bend, just across from the tiny footbridge crossing the stream to the council houses beyond . . . Fifteen. A young age to die. But what age was the right one to meet one's Maker?

The neighbour had been informative and chatty, her Devonian accent almost a caricature coming from rosy lips, and the disapproving expression emerging from apple cheeks and bright blue eyes. It was clear she did not care for her neighbour Mrs Park; it was equally clear she was very interested to discover what the tall, bony stranger wanted with her. She hinted that maybe Crow was an insurance agent; he did not disabuse her and managed to obtain the information that if Marlene Park was anywhere, she'd be down in the Miner's Arms with her usual crowd. A sniff accompanied the statement; the neighbour with the apple cheeks disapproved of the company Marlene kept.

There were, surprisingly, only about ten cars in the car park; Crow had assumed the inn would have been more crowded at lunchtime. He made the comment to the landlord when he had ordered a half-pint of lager in the lounge bar, which held only half-a-dozen people.

'Market day up at Tilhampton,' the landlord explained. 'And there's a fair over by Tavistock, too. So 'tis quiet, apart from the regulars.'

The rumble of a passing lorry made the windows tremble; Crow looked around at the people in the lounge bar. They were youngsters, mainly, heads close together as they sat on dark oak settles near the empty fireplace, apart from the elderly couple who sat silently, black-coated, near the display of horse brasses winking on the wall. The landlord polished a beer glass with a vigorous motion and caught Crow's eye. He nodded towards the old couple. 'Every day. Never say a word. Since before my time 'ere. But regular as clockwork.'

'I've just been up the hill,' Crow said, 'looking for one of your regular patrons.'

'Up at Portworthy Cottages? Who'd you be lookin' for up there, then?'

'Mrs Park. I was told she was probably down here . . . with some friends.'

The landlord's broad face closed professionally; the barman's mask was one Crow had seen many times over the years, a careful impassivity that was as controlled as the laughing bonhomie that could be assumed for old patrons. He turned away, putting back the beer glass, 'Aye, she's been in here this morning. You . . . er . . . you'd be wantin' to see her, then?'

'Is she in the other bar?'

The landlord shook his head and nodded towards the back of the building. 'No. Mrs Park's back there. Committee meeting.'

'Committee?'

'Ottershaw Action Committee.' The landlord ran the back of a questing hand under his nose, and sniffed. 'They meet here at least once a week.'

His tone told Crow nothing; perhaps the man disapproved of the committee and its objectives, but it *was* custom for his pub.

'What time are they likely to finish?' Crow asked.

The landlord glanced at the clock on the wall. 'Give 'em ten minutes, and Jack Prince'll be breaking it up. He'll want 'is pint — particularly if he can get one of the committee to buy it for him.' The man hesitated, glancing at Crow quizzically. 'I could go in and tell Marlene you're here, Mr . . . er . . .'

Crow smiled and shook his head. 'I'll wait until the meeting breaks up. No hurry.' He took his glass of lager and walked across the room to a seat near the window. The window was blurry, with a fine white dust on the outside, the residue of the heavy traffic through the village. He sipped his lager and waited.

When the Ottershaw Action Committee emerged into the lounge bar ten minutes later, as the landlord had predicted, Crow had time to look them over, weigh them up as a group. They were seven in number, and familiar in type. There were four women and three men. Two of the women were middle-aged, a third rather elderly, in tweeds. One of the men looked like a bank manager and was probably an estate agent, Crow guessed, eager to protect his business interests, and the second man had a blimpish appearance, with flying moustaches and brown walking boots — pretensions to class without the class to realize they were pretensions, Crow thought waspishly.

The other two, the man and the woman standing at the bar, he had seen before. They were the couple he had seen involved in the altercation with the lorry-driver in the main street, the day he had arrived in Ottershaw.

She was wearing a red sweater today, but it outlined her figure as boldly as had the white one she had affected when Crow first saw her, and though she wore a skirt rather than trousers on this occasion, it fitted so closely over the hips that her movements remained as obviously provocative as before. She was laughing at something one of her companions was saying, and it was a throaty, affected laugh, calculated to express her femininity and sexuality. She had a hand on her companion's shoulder as she whispered something to him, and he threw back his head to laugh loudly at her comment.

He wore a tweed jacket today, and a white open-necked shirt; it seemed to make him look even more powerful than the donkey jacket he had worn earlier. He had half-turned from the woman now, and was talking to the bank manager/estate agent; the woman was leaning forward as the landlord said something to her in a quiet tone, and nodded in Crow's direction. She turned her head to stare at Crow, and even at this distance he was aware of her surprise as she took in his appearance. She leaned with her back to the bar and stared at him boldly, sipping her gin and tonic; he met her glance indifferently and waited. After a little while she said something to her companion, who brushed the remark aside, and then she swayed across towards the window-seat where John Crow waited.

She stood in front of him, her eyes bold and challenging. 'I hear you're asking about me.'

'Mrs Park?'

That's right.'

'My name is Crow. Detective Superintendent Crow.' Fear came sudden, dancing and flickering across her face, eradicating the boldness from her eyes and slackening her mouth. He was aware of the network of fine lines around her eyes as she said,

'What . . . what do you want with me?'

'I merely wanted to ask you a few questions. There's no need for alarm.'

'Alarm?' Some of the confidence came bouncing back into her features. 'I got nothing to be scared of.' But she cast an involuntary glance over her shoulder to the man at the bar, as though wanting his support. His back was to her; he did not catch the suppliant gesture.

'Would you like to sit down, Mrs Park? I should explain,' Crow continued as the woman hesitantly took the seat he offered, placing the gin and tonic on the table in front of her. 'I'm merely filling in some background on the Norman case.'

'Fred Norman?' The panic was back in her eyes briefly, before she reached forward and sipped her gin. 'I don't know a thing about that business.'

'I'm sure that's so,' Crow said soothingly, 'but you must understand we need to piece together all his movements and . . . involvements during the period before his death. And I gather you had some contact with him.'

'Who told you that?' she asked sharply. When Crow made no reply she cast another unavailing glance towards the bar and went on, 'It depends what you mean by contact. I . . . I met him a few times, with the others. It was on account of the campaign.'

'Your Action Committee?'

'That's right. We was meeting this morning. He . . . he came to a couple of our meetings. To hear the point of view us was putting to him.' She looked again towards the bar, and this time her imploring glance obtained a response. The man in the open-necked shirt picked up his beer and shouldered his way past his companions to walk across the room. He stood in front of Crow and Marlene Park, his heavy eyebrows ridged, a hint of belligerency about his mouth.

'Jack, this is Detective Superintendent Crow.'

He was more in control of his expression than the woman; there was a tightening of the muscles around his mouth, nothing more. 'So what's he want with you, then?'

'He's asking about Fred Norman's death.'

Jack Prince's head jutted forward and he waved his beer glass in a vaguely contemptuous manner. 'Better spending his time finding who killed your kid.'

'I'm not sure—' Crow began, but Prince interrupted him with a growing belligerence.

'It's bloody typical, isn't it! An American company moves into the area and everyone has to start jumpin' through hoops! There's our bloody MP, Foster: he's running around with his shirt-tails out, suckin' up to this Streisman bloke. There's all the talk of hundreds of jobs, but all the good jobs on that site are going to Streisman men they draft into the area. They keep sayin' they are concerned about the bloody environment, but at the same time those damned lorries come chargin' through the main street and the plans are to treble the number, and to hell with the people who live here!'

'Do you live in the village, Mr Prince?' Crow asked.

There was a blur of surprise in the man's eyes. 'You know my name?' he asked, and then, as he glanced at Marlene Park and understood that rumour had preceded him, the surprise was replaced by anger. 'Aye, I live around here. Up in Portworthy Cottages, as you'll no doubt have heard already. But that's typical too . . . people will talk readily enough, but will they do anything when there's something important to be done? Will they hell! If it wasn't for the Action Committee the whole village would be taking this business lying down. If it wasn't for Marlene and me—'

'You're the mainsprings behind the campaign, I've heard that,' Crow said mildly. 'And I gather you had some dealings with Mr Norman as a result. That's why—'

'Dealings? Aye, we had dealings with the bastard. And he wouldn't move! But it's like I was saying: none of you gives a damn unless there's somebody with *money* behind it all. Just because Norman was a Streisman man you all come tumbling out of your holes to find the bloke who done him in. But it's a different story when it's a kid knocked down in the street!'

Crow looked at Marlene Park. 'Yes, I'd heard about your daughter, Mrs Park. I'm sorry. Accidents of that kind—'

Jack Prince banged his beer glass down on the table between Crow and Marlene Park. 'Bein' sorry isn't good enough. You coppers, you make me sick. Somebody *killed* that girl, and no serious attempt's been made to find out who. But with the death of a Streisman employee . . .' His eyebrows drew together in a sudden suspicion. 'You're not a local copper, are you?'

Crow shook his head. 'Murder Squad.'

'There you are,' Prince said triumphantly. 'Proves it. They'll draft in outside help for the Norman case, but ignore Freda's death. I told you Marlene, these bastards, all they're concerned about is—'

'I take it,' Crow said with ice in his tone, 'your conversations with Fred Norman were along these lines.'

Jack Prince glared at him. His mouth was suddenly pinched, as though he wished he had been able to withdraw some of the words he had used. 'Fred Norman? He . . . he didn't want to know.'

'He was responsible for dealing with all environmental problems. This was a police matter — a hit-and-run case — but I imagine you'll have spoken to him as you spoke to me.'

'Too bloody true!'

'I also understand he made extensive enquiries among Streisman transport—'

'And found damn all!' Prince interrupted. 'A whitewash job, of course: I mean, they weren't going to *admit* that one of their drivers knocked Freda down and killed her that evening! Stands to reason Norman would protect—'

'That's not the impression I've received,' Crow said quietly.

'I don't give a damn for your impressions,' Prince said in a grinding tone. 'All we know is that the girl was killed, and the chances are it was a Streisman lorry, but because it *is* Streisman the police hush it up and put no muscle into it, and Fred Norman does damn all, and everything goes on as before — except we won't stand for it! We're getting outside help now, and we'll make this bloody corporation sit up before long, I promise you.'

'What makes you so certain the hit-and-run was a Streisman driver?' Crow asked.

Prince picked up his beer glass contemptuously and drained it. 'Stands to reason. No lorries come through from Lewforth late at night. There's still the odd Streisman vehicle, though. I'm sure it was that bloody company.' He glowered at Crow defiantly. 'I know it was them that was responsible.'

Crow hesitated. Prince's belligerent attitude had ignited a slow fuse of anger, which he was trying to control. Almost in spite of himself, the words came out. 'Where were you, Mrs Park, when your daughter was killed?' In the short silence that followed, Crow added, 'I mean, what was she doing out alone at ten at night?'

The silence lengthened; spots of colour burned angrily m Marlene Park's face. Her eyes were hostile, her mouth twisting with unspoken obscenities. 'I was a good mother, I was. If I couldn't just go down for a drink in the evening—'

Jack Prince grasped her upper arm and pulled her to her feet. In a rasping voice, he said, 'We don't have to listen to insinuations like that. You got nothing to be guilty about; nothin' to answer for. We don't have to answer questions like this.'

Crow shook his head. 'Not about Freda Park's death I agree. I'm only interested in the murder of Fred Norman — and I'm seeking to establish whether the quarrel you had with him was over the matter you've been talking about now, or whether it was something else.'

'Quarrel?' Prince stood rigidly, his angry self-confidence ebbing away for the first time. 'Who says I quarrelled with Norman?'

'I'm told,' Crow remarked mildly, 'that some sort of quarrel broke out in this inn, between you and Norman, shortly before his death.'

A tremor ran through Marlene Park's body. Prince was aware of it, and he tightened his grip on her arm, his fingers white against the red of her sweater. 'There's no way you can try to tie me in with Fred Norman's death,' he said thickly.

'But you *did* quarrel with him?' Prince made a vaguely derogatory movement with his left hand; it could have been dissent, but Crow went on, 'And I presume it had to do with the hit-and-run . . . or was it merely the village street issue?'

Jack Prince stood staring at Crow for several seconds in complete silence. The lounge bar itself was quiet; Prince's raised voice had drawn attention to the group near the window, and the committee members at the bar were openly watching for developments. Abruptly Jack Prince released Marlene Park's arm. 'Siddown,' he said to her. 'You want another drink?'

Before she could reply he marched off towards the bar and ordered another pint of beer and a gin and tonic. As he waited to be served, Marlene Park cautiously slid into the seat opposite Crow again. Her face was marked with a fog of incomprehension, as though she could not understand what was happening to her, and why. It might have been memories of her daughter's death, but Crow, even on such short acquaintance, was inclined to support the theory advanced by Alan Fairfield — the woman had thrown herself into the Ottershaw village campaign partly because of her own feelings of guilt regarding her daughter's death. It was a guilt Jack Prince would not allow to surface openly, nevertheless.

Prince thrust the gin and tonic in front of her carelessly, so that it spilled. He took a drink from his own glass and then sat down beside the woman. 'All right,' he said to Crow, 'I had a quarrel with Fred Norman.'

In the interval while he had been getting the drinks he had had time to think, and compose himself. He was in control again, whereas under Crow's earlier questioning he had been on the brink of possibly dangerous admissions. There would be no such admissions now.

'What was the quarrel about?' Crow asked.

'You've already guessed. It wasn't often Norman came in here, but on this occasion, even though there was no committee meeting, he came looking for me and Marlene. You see, he'd attended one meeting where we'd spoken plainly and said we thought his company was responsible for Freda's death. He said he'd look further into it. This night he came in and he was . . . categorical. He'd gone through all the schedules and mileages and everything else, he said: the company was clean. No Streisman lorry was in the vicinity that night. Freda hadn't been killed by a Streisman employee.'

'What was your reaction to that?' Crow asked, already guessing at the answer.

'I blew my top. At least . . . well, it wasn't just that. I told him I didn't believe him, that he was just doing a whitewash job. I mean, it's too easy, isn't it?'

'The police would seem to have been satisfied,' Crow suggested mildly.

Prince's mouth curled unpleasantly. 'You know what I think of *their* commitment. Anyway, when I told him I didn't believe him, Norman got a bit excited. I admit, too, I'd had a few pints, and maybe I said things I shouldn't have.' The edge of humility in his tone grated on Crow for its insincerity, but he made no comment as Prince went on. 'It was only when he said he thought I was using the hit-and-run incident for the purpose of whipping up support for the village campaign that I saw red. Marlene knows better than that. Freda . . . she was . . . it was just like she was my own, you know? And when that bastard Norman said that, I lost my temper. I lunged at him—'

'He didn't hit him,' Marlene Park said nervously. 'Jack was pretty drunk, and a couple of the lads held him back, until Mr Norman had a chance to get out of there. You can ask the landlord about that. Jack was swearing and shouting, but it was just noise, you know? Nothing more than that. It wasn't really a quarrel, not the kind you're suggesting.'

'*I'm* suggesting nothing, Mrs Park. I'm just trying to establish some facts. But . . . er . . . why should Mr Norman think you'd use your daughter's death to whip up support for the campaign? I mean, what motives did he impute to you?'

There was a short silence. Jack Prince stared at his beer. Finally, it was Marlene Park who spoke, and for the first time in his observation of their relationship Crow realized she was a stronger partner than he had suspected. Till now a certain anxiety had robbed her of strength, and Prince had seemed the dominant individual; but now there were hints that she possessed a steel Crow had not realized. 'Jack is going places,' she said coldly. 'There are people who don't like that; people who are jealous. He was doing well over at Lewforth until the management trumped up charges against him to get rid of him. He was too tough for them, too strong — so they gave him the push. And now he can swing this campaign, because he's got ideas, Jack has, and the strength and determination to carry them through. I'm right behind him, and if Freda's death . . . if Freda's death can help, then she didn't die in vain. Those bastards . . .' Her eyes were glistening; Crow could not be certain whether it was the result of sorrow or self-pity. 'Fred Norman was scared, that's why he started saying what he did. He came along and said what the bosses told him to say, and because Jack wouldn't take it, he lost his head. And that's how the quarrel started. They're afraid of Jack, the Streisman company are. He's raising support, not just around here, but up at Exeter, and even Bristol, too. He went up there—'

'There's a lot of people don't want that mine opened,' Prince interrupted. 'There's enough spoil about here, and I've convinced the South-Western Activists that this is one they can win.'

Crow had heard of the group. Anarchic, youthful, but financed by some wealthy backers, they were committed to keeping the south-west of England unscarred as a holiday area. He could understand Norman's suggestion that Prince was out for something for himself. If the man was able to involve the Activist group, money would flow in his direction. And yet, perhaps these thoughts were uncharitable: Prince and the mother of the dead girl *could* be sincere. He sighed. 'All right. So you say the quarrel wasn't an important one. That it would carry no animosity between you thereafter. In that case, perhaps you wouldn't mind telling me, Mr Prince, where you were on the night that Fred Norman was murdered. Can you account for your movements?'

Prince sent one flickering glance towards Marlene Park before he replied, as though he wished he'd been able to say he was with her. Then he said, 'I wasn't even in the area; not even near Ottershaw. I'd gone up to Bristol to see the Activists — I stayed overnight and came back middle of the next afternoon. Marlene met me off the bus, from Plymouth.'

His eyes were wide, pleading honesty; his mouth touched with sincerity. Crow felt that if he reached out a hand he could wipe both away with a touch.

* * *

Delaval joined Crow at the pilot plant site that afternoon, but they worked separately, Delaval going over contract details with Ray Grainger, who reluctantly agreed to open up files he held regarding the road plans west of the Leveson estates, and to contact headquarters at Exeter to clear access for Delaval to the Leveson agreements generally, the court proceedings that were projected, and the planning enquiry evidences that were being prepared. Crow himself had a long conversation with Norman's former secretary, Janet, but was able to elicit little further information from her. She showed him all Norman's files now held by O'Connor, and she listed for him the report — which Norman had filed of recent months. He picked up Norman's work diary and inspected the contents. There were two entries that now interested him, and he decided to follow them up immediately. Explaining to Janet that he would call back to see her later in the afternoon, he made his way with the diary to Ray Grainger's office.

Delaval was with Grainger when he entered. Crow decided to come straight to the point.

'Inspector Delaval, you told me last night over dinner that your conversation with Brigadier Leveson led you to believe the last occasion on which he saw Norman was . . .'

'Six to eight weeks ago,' Delaval said.

Crow turned to Ray Grainger. His eyes were as earnest and eager to help as ever Delaval had suggested. 'Did Norman keep accurate work diaries?' Crow asked abruptly.

'I've no reason to believe otherwise,' Grainger replied.

Crow handed him the diary. 'It would seem from this entry that Norman visited Brigadier Leveson a matter of two days before his death.'

Grainger stared at the entry. He was silent for a little while. Then he handed the book back with a shrug. 'I suppose Leveson could have made a mistake.'

'Does he have any reason you can think of for being evasive?'

'I've no idea what goes on in the Brigadier's mind,' Grainger snapped, near to sudden explosion. 'I've no idea why he should fail to tell you about that visit, but Fred certainly said nothing to me. But he had his own job to do; it wasn't his way to come running to me with his problems. I've enough of my own.'

Crow nodded. 'So he said nothing to you about carrying out checks, or making a report of some kind on Leveson, or his activities.'

'Nothing. A report—'

'Janet tells me Norman was working on some kind of report in the days before he died. She doesn't know about what, and for whom. But this diary entry *might* mean that Norman was preparing a report on Leveson, and went to see him about it shortly before he died.'

Crow was aware of Delaval staring at him in surprise.

He half-smiled, realizing that the young inspector considered Crow had taken a step before the bridge was laid. 'I'm only trying to lend support to your feelings that Leveson's actions and motives might bear closer scrutiny. Have you had the clearances from the Exeter office?'

Delaval nodded. 'And Mr Grainger has told me a bit more about Brigadier Leveson's . . . ah . . . decision to resile from the agreements reached by his predecessor in title.'

'Why is he backing out from his *uncle's* contract?' Crow asked, aware of Delaval's discomfiture at attention being drawn to his stilted legal language.

'I don't know *that,'* Grainger said in exasperation, 'but I was explaining that Leveson's point of view isn't the only one. I don't think he stands a cat in hell's chance of breaking that agreement his uncle made. At best all he can do is delay us and cost us a few hundred thousand in cash and a lot of trouble through broken relationships in the village. Why the hell *that* should be important to him, I don't know. But our lawyers feel he can't break the options and will have to allow them — they're legal. We'll ask for specific performance of that agreement.'

'And the later agreement, with Leveson himself?' Grainger looked vaguely embarrassed. He passed a hand over his mouth as though to wipe away the emotion.

'That was Fred's idea, and I went along with it because it would be normal practice anyway. There would have been certain difficulties as a result of the contours of the land over the tongue, but I thought it worth the extra outlay just to keep Leveson quiet and get his agreement to the options without fuss. But, well, Myron Streisman wouldn't have seen it that way. *He* would have said Leveson is indulging in moral blackmail, and would have refused to ratify the proposal. It was left to Fred to break the news — and I gather Leveson thought he'd been conned.'

'By Norman?'

Grainger shrugged. 'Maybe he does personalize things.'

Delaval expressed a certain doubt. 'I'm still not certain Brigadier Leveson feels a wronged man — not to the extent of pursuing causes as lost as the ones you suggest.'

'He'll lose all right,' Grainger said stubbornly.

Crow nodded to Delaval; the young man would do the plodding bit there. He himself had another question to raise.

He left the office and walked out to the main site once more. For a little while he watched lorries stopping at the main gate, and then he walked over to the tailings pond again, to stare at its murky surface as though it yet held secrets to impart. Then, after a while, he made his way to Alan Fairfield's office.

The Transport Manager was in his shirt-sleeves and obviously somewhat exasperated. He was not unhappy to see Crow: it meant a break from work that was displeasing him. He explained that at a morning meeting he'd been given the task of arranging transport and accommodation for a number of important people arriving for the formal opening of the pilot plant in a week's time. It was going to raise considerable difficulties for him: to start with, the fleet of cars he would have expected to hire easily enough would now have to be arranged from Bristol, because of pressures raised by a royal visit to Exeter. Secondly, he still had to work out a route that would cause least inconvenience to visitors, which was difficult in view of the problems at Ottershaw village. Thirdly, Myron Streisman would be arriving with the supportive MP, Foster — by helicopter. That meant not only the provision of a suitable landing site — which would have to be at the pilot plant — but, in addition, appropriate security arrangements which were demanded by the Home Office for the Minister. 'And last, but by no means least,' Fairfield growled, 'I've got a funny feeling about this one.'

'How do you mean?'

'I was down at the Miner's Arms last night. I sensed . . . a certain atmosphere when I walked in. A few conversations stopped. I think trouble's brewing.'

'And you think it might come to a head on the day of the formal opening?'

Fairfield spread his hands in a helpless gesture. 'Can you imagine the chaos it would cause if only Myron Streisman and the Minister arrived — with everyone else ground to a halt in an Ottershaw village traffic jam? There'd be hell to pay, and I know whose head would be on the block. But,' he added with a weary sigh, 'I got my problems, no doubt you got yours. You wanted a word?'

Crow nodded and sat down in front of Fairfield, leaned forward with one bony elbow on the desk. 'It's in connection with the village problem, really. I've seen Marlene Park and her friend Prince.'

Fairfield made no reply immediately, but his glance became restless. 'What did they have to say?' he asked at last.

'They confirmed what you told me, about the quarrel with Fred Norman. And a few other things. But . . . er . . . how do you know about them, anyway?'

'Local gossip. I rent a couple of rooms down at the village, you see. And I drink in the Miner's Arms from time to time. I suppose I'm more accepted at the village than any of the outsiders who work up here. I've been there a couple of years, after all, and I've got to know most people living in the village. And Marlene Park — well, I've been in company with her and Prince a few times, though that was way back really, before things got nasty down there.'

'Did you know the daughter — the one that was killed?'

'By sight.' Fairfield hesitated, seeming to be about to say something, but reconsidering, thinking better of it. 'She . . . I saw her a few times in the village, and once or twice when the pub turned out.'

'You mean she often came down to the Miner's Arms?'

Fairfield hesitated again, and his eyes roamed the room as though seeking an answer. 'Look, I don't know, but I think she used to come down to walk home with her mother and Prince. That's what she'll have been doing the night she was killed. Probably came out just before ten, walked down — and then was struck by the hit-and-run.'

'Jack Prince thinks — no, is certain — that the driver was a Streisman man.'

'I know it.'

'But you don't subscribe to it?'

Fairfield shook his head positively. 'No way I can. Look, Superintendent, I've already told you why, in my view, Prince and Mrs Park are shoving the line they are. But we had to check it out. The police came out and did their own check, but — you'll forgive me — our own check was a damn sight more painstaking. I told you, Fred and I went over the whole thing months ago. Here, I'll show you.' He rose and walked across to a filing cabinet standing against the wall. He opened the second drawer and extracted several files, brought them to the desk and opened the top one. 'You're welcome to go through these yourself, but all you'll find is the kind of confirmation we found. Fred and I went through the lot with great care. These consist of two records: the jobs Streisman vehicles were on at particular times, day by day — so they constitute a complete work schedule for each vehicle — and a record of the mileage run up-which can be double-checked on the vehicles themselves, of course. Then, in this file here, you'll see the drivers' schedules, day by day. Once again, a double check can be run against the vehicles to which they're assigned.'

'And you did the double-checking?'

Fairfield smiled wryly. 'Fred Norman was a very methodical man.'

Crow browsed through the records for a few minutes while Fairfield watched him. There seemed to be no discrepancies in the account Fairfield had given him. Crow put Norman's working diary on the desk. 'According to this entry here, and on subsequent pages, Norman spent several days travelling the county a few days before his death. He was visiting local garages.' He looked up at Fairfield. 'Do you know why he would be doing that?'

Fairfield scratched his cheek and nodded, sighing. 'I told you, Fred was a methodical man. He always tied up all ends. Yeah, he visited the garages. The fact is, he went to every garage which has a connection or a contract with Streisman, and looked through their books.'

'For what reason?'

'It was just after his argument with Jack Prince. He was upset; I think he felt that Prince's anger might have some foundation. He knew he'd checked all our records here so he then did this further check.'

'The objective?'

'To discover whether any of our vehicles had been taken into any of these garages for repairs, resprays, anything of that kind. To cover up damage done in a hit-and-run accident.'

'The result?'

Fairfield shook his head. 'What you might expect. A great big zero. I mean, the police had already done it, so the chances were slim anyway. But, methodical as he was, he plodded around and did it. For nothing. Except, maybe, salving his own conscience, in the sense he could be categorical about his statements to Jack Prince and Marlene Park.'

'Did he put this in a report?' Crow asked.

'Report?' Fairfield's glance was guarded. 'What do you mean?'

'Fred Norman seems to have been pretty busy the couple of weeks before his death. He went to see Brigadier

Leveson. He went, for some reason we don't yet know, to Exeter. He did a tour of the garages. And it seems he was preparing some kind of report. No one can tell me what the report was about. I just wondered—'

'He made a verbal report to me about the garages check,' Fairfield said, 'but there was no question of getting anything in writing. He was checking for his own purposes, to verify what he already believed to be true. The report he was working on had nothing to do with transport.'

'You seem very positive about that,' Crow said, watching him closely.

'I am.'

'Do you know what he *was* working on, then?'

For just one moment something flared in Fairfield's eyes and he was on the point of saying something. Then the light faded and died, and the Transport Manager shook his head, saying nothing.

But Crow was left with the feeling that the man knew more than he was saying.

* * *

Within the hour it seemed less important than Crow thought. He had another session with Janet, and as they went through the files together she was thinking hard. When he asked her whether it was likely that Fred Norman had been working on a report regarding transport she shook her head positively.

'No, it certainly wasn't that. He'd been spending time with Mr Fairfield but . . . no, wait a minute, I'm sure it was something to do with the drilling. That was it . . . the drilling work being done by the sub-contractors!'

'Craydon Engineering?'

'That's right,' she said, beaming widely with relief, a good secretary earning her money. 'He'd been checking some of their figures and . . . and I'm pretty sure he'd discussed them with Mr Harris.'

Pete Harris was in conference with Ray Grainger and, reluctant to disturb the Project Manager yet again, Crow went to Harris's office and waited there for him. Harris's secretary brought him a cup of tea, and he sat there in the warm room, his long bony legs crossed at the ankles, seemingly relaxed, but with his brain still churning over what he had learned. He felt deflated in a curious way, even though he felt he was close to discovering what Norman had been working on just before his death. The identity, the character, the personality of Fred Norman seemed as distant from him now as it had ever been. Normally, in the course of an investigation into a death, Crow felt, perhaps fancifully, that he got to know the murdered person, came close to understanding him as layers of fact were peeled away to reveal human feelings and reactions and motivations. But up till now he saw Norman in an oddly automotive light. Methodical, persistent, dogged, probably lonely and uncomplaining, but almost secretive during his last weeks. Was that secretiveness part of his character, or had it been forced upon him by circumstance? And if the latter — what kind of circumstance?

His musings were disturbed by Pete Harris's entrance. Harris made no attempt to conceal his surprise; his fleshy mouth dropped open, and his flint-coloured eyes widened. 'Oh. Superintendent Crow. I hadn't expected to see you here. You've got some tea, I see.' He asked his secretary to make a cup for him, and as he settled behind his desk he began to grumble about the interminable meetings he had to attend. He was, he explained, far more interested in and committed to the exploration work outside, and he did not care for the paperwork that was demanded of him.

'I suppose that must come with your position, surely?' Crow asked.

'That's right.' The soft mouth moved, a hint of pride creeping into his voice. 'When Myron Streisman called me to his office he told me that this was the chance of a lifetime for me. You'll appreciate I'm pretty young to be holding down an exploration job of this magnitude. I mean, eight million pounds . . . So I shouldn't gripe about the desk work, really. After all, when we establish the commercial viability of the mine, in professional terms the sky will be the limit for me.'

'*When* the commercial viability is established?'

'There's no doubt in my mind that it will be so established,' Harris replied seriously. 'We still have some technical problems to sort out in the laboratory, but we can master them, I'm certain. I've been doing some research on a newly developed type of spiral — the Budin spiral concentrator — which has been used on scheelite ores in Turkey. And then there's the Chinese rocking-shaking vanner — it's a new gravity concentrating device — which I think has distinct possibilities for us. After all, we *know* the wolframite is there: if we can only perfect our lab techniques during the next couple of years . . . I mean, there's the use of photometric ore-sorters to be investigated as well—'

'You're pretty certain you'll come up with the right answers.'

'Positive.'

'And as you say, the wolframite *is* there — as long as you can get it out without destroying the environment,' Crow said quietly.

Harris looked at him, the corners of his mouth turning down petulantly. 'That's not my concern.'

'As I understood the policy of the Streisman Corporation,' Crow countered, 'it's the concern of every employee on the site — and a major concern, at that.'

That's not quite what I meant,' Harris conceded. 'I meant that my task is exploration matters: O'Connor deals with environmental considerations as his major involvement.'

'And before him, it was Fred Norman.' Crow paused. 'I presume the report he was preparing for you concerned some form of environmental problem that arose from your exploration activities on the site?'

Harris licked his fleshy lips and looked puzzled. 'Report? I don't believe—'

Patiently Crow explained. 'I imagine you'll remember our meeting in Grainger's conference. You told me then you didn't know what Norman had been working on during, the last weeks before he died. Though you also said you'd probably worked more closely with him than anyone else on site would have.'

'That's true.'

'So why didn't you mention the report he was preparing for you?' Crow asked.

Harris's eyes were bland, but there was a hint of anger in the line of his mouth. 'I'm afraid you're misinformed. Fred was preparing no report for me.'

Crow regarded him carefully for a few seconds. 'You're positive about that?'

'Absolutely.'

A short silence fell. At last Crow said, 'I've just been speaking to Janet, Norman's secretary.' He finished the tea in his cup before going on. 'She told me Norman *had* been working on a report. She couldn't remember for whom It had been intended. A few minutes ago she said she thought it had been for you.'

'For me?' The furrows on his brow were delicately etched, carefully arranged. 'I don't think that's correct.'

'Well, If not for you,' Crow conceded, 'she seems to recall that he had discussed them with you. Statistics of some kind, she said.'

Slowly Pete Harris shook his head. 'Janet must be mistaken. I don't recall . . .' John Crow had seen it often enough before, the clearing of doubts, the raising of a memory curtain, the dawning of clarity over a misty fog of forgetfulness. He had seen it and never believed it; he saw it now. The furrows were smoothed on Harris's brow; the fleshy mouth smiled while the eyes remained watchful. 'Now wait a minute . . .'

'Yes?' Crow said politely.

'She has got it wrong!' Harris said triumphantly. 'She's got her lines crossed a bit, though it's understandable enough. When you said he was preparing a report for me I didn't focus on it distinctly. I've got more than enough on my mind, as you might imagine.'

'Quite so. But—'

'He wasn't preparing a report for me,' Harris interjected. 'He'd already submitted one. That's where the slip-up was, really. I just wasn't thinking.'

The room was silent as Crow waited. Harris obviously expected Crow to make the next move, so the superintendent smiled, and said, 'Ah well, that clears up things. But what was the report about?'

'Oh, it was just company exploration matters of a technical nature.'

'And specifically-?'

'I'm not sure I should divulge private reports to—'

'Mr Harris! I'm the soul of discretion. And if you doubt whether you should give it to me, check with Ray Grainger — or for that matter Myron Streisman himself.'

The name of the head of Streisman Corporation brought a confused pallor to Harris's cheeks. The flinty points of light appeared in his eyes, reflections of uncertainty. 'Well, I suppose it'll be all right.' He rose, walked to the filing cabinet, unlocked it, and after a little while drew out a file. He passed it to John Crow.

It was a spiral-bound, card-covered booklet containing about thirty sheets of close typing. Crow turned the sheets slowly, flicking through the contents. Pete Harris shuffled some papers on his desk, uneasily. 'I can summarize it for you, if you wish.'

'That would be useful,' Crow said.

'The genesis of this work was that I asked Fred Norman to carry out a study for me — as you know, the mining here at Ottershaw will be by conventional open pit methods. The shape of the ore body determines the pit shape—'

'One moment. Does that mean that the open pit would not necessarily be worked as a series of concentric circles?'

Harris shrugged. 'It could. But in this case, as you'll see, Fred pointed out that the pit shape will be irregular, a sort of flattened circle, with a flattening in the west, with a spiral haul road. Anyway, he produced in this report data which followed from certain assumptions I'd given him: namely, that we'd be using small equipment of the order of 6-yard front-end loaders, such as CAT 988Bs; that 30 to 50-tonne trucks would produce a proposed two million tonne per year ore output, and that benches would be about five yards, and blast-holes four inches. Then there was the accessory equipment, such as CAT D8 'dozers, and regarding pit stability—'

'Yes, I see,' Crow said, somewhat dazed by the technical data thrown at him by the Exploration Manager. 'Well, I'll look carefully at the report — I may take it away, of course?'

Harris pursed his lips, hesitated, then shrugged. 'I suppose so. It's not really a secret, after all. Company property, of course, but in the circumstances . . .'

'When was this report prepared?' Crow asked, turning to the front cover.

'I believe it's stated there,' Harris said casually. Just at the foot of the first sheet.'

Crow noted it: *FN 16 Feb.* He looked up at Harris. 'He completed this just a few days before he died, then?'

'That's right. His body was found on February 20, I believe.'

Crow stared at Pete Harris, and the young Exploration Manager met his glance steadily. A vague sense of disappointment touched Crow, but it was backed also by a niggling feeling that he had missed something.

It was this general uneasiness that made him go back to Janet, Norman's ex-secretary, before he left the site to return to his hotel. He had only one question to ask her. 'Did Mr Harris have access to Mr Norman's work diary?'

Janet fluttered a little before answering, nervously, that he would not normally have access to it. 'But . . . but in the days after Mr Norman died there was such a fuss going on, and no one seemed to know what was happening . . . we were all in a state of shock, you understand . . . I believe Mr Harris did come in to ask me if he could see the work diary. He just looked quickly through it, as I remember. And he . . . he took it all so hard, poor young man. He was very disturbed, Superintendent, very disturbed by Mr Norman's death. I can still see his face now: he was very pale, very strained. And that was days after poor Mr Norman's body was found. It seemed to hit Mr Harris harder than anyone.'

There were tears in her eyes once more when John Crow left. He himself was wondering, however, whether Harris's concern had been merely connected with the loss of his colleague, or whether there was something else . . .

But for the moment he could not pin down in his mind the vague, fluttering doubt that bothered him.

* * *

Crow spent the next morning at headquarters in Exeter, working on files they had compiled during the early days of the investigation into Norman's death. Crow guessed there had been a certain degree of confusion at the time; inexperienced officers would seem to have been involved before a detective superintendent called Carr had been assigned to the case, three days after the body had been found.

Carr himself seemed affable enough when Crow asked if he could spare time for a chat. He was a burly, balding Devonian with huge hands and a creased face that suggested he laughed often, but his affability was presently tempered, for all that, by the resentment Crow knew would be simmering just below the surface. Crow began by paying some veiled compliments to the man on the way he had pulled the investigation together after the initial mistakes; veiled, because he knew Carr would resent even more strongly anything he saw as patronizing or ingratiating. Thereafter, Crow spent some time discussing the forensic report with him, and invited the local man's views.

'Well,' Carr said slowly, 'it seems to me the killer would have been someone known to Norman. Let's take the report from the forensic boys at Bristol. It tells us that there were few signs of violence on the body. Three blows to the head — the first one probably stunned him, put him to his knees; the second smashed the back of his skull, drove splinters of bone into the brain, and effectively killed him; the third was delivered probably when he was hitting the ground, almost a glancing blow.' Carr took out a pipe and filled it, lit up before continuing. 'After that, if we assume the murder did not take place at the plant site, he was loaded into a vehicle and driven along that access road towards the tailings pond.'

'Why the tailings pond?'

Carr drew on his pipe thoughtfully. 'Not sure about that. The murderer would know, obviously, that the sludge would effectively hide the body — but so would the moors. I reckon he chose the pond rather than the moors because it was easier, swifter — no grave to dig — and, maybe, his presence at the site would not be observed.'

'Observed,' Crow said softly, 'in the sense that there would be nothing unusual in his being there? In other words, you think the killer is someone who works at the site.'

'I reckon,' Carr said blandly.

'All right, it's a hypothesis,' Crow said noncommittally. 'What about motive?'

Carr watched the blue smoke from his pipe laze its way to the ceiling. He scratched the side of his nose with the pipe stem. 'Can't give you any help on that.'

'You didn't have any theories to work on?'

'Didn't have time to develop any,' Carr replied.

There was a short, uneasy silence. Crow stared at the Devonian, who avoided his glance. 'I hope you'll appreciate that this wasn't my idea,' Crow said quietly.

Carr shrugged. 'You're here. It's your pigeon now.'

'I understand your . . . feelings. I pointed them out to . . . to the people who insisted the Murder Squad be drafted in.'

Carr made an angry gesture with his pipe. 'Ah, the Chief Constable should've—'

'I don't think he had much choice, either,' Crow interrupted. 'Political pressure was brought; that's pretty difficult to fight off.'

'Humph! And I can guess who put the screws on the politicians!' Carr's eyes were brown, and soft, but they were shadowed now by suppressed anger. 'I tell you, Crow, we're all getting pretty fed up around here with the way this Streisman chap is turning everybody upside down, just as though he owns the bloody county! All right, so he comes breezing in and says he's going to set up three hundred jobs and more; all right, he's going to do something big for the national economy! But why Whitehall and our bloody MP, Foster, have to fall over backwards just because a Yank makes a few easy promises, I don't understand! We never needed Streisman, anyway!'

'How do you mean?'

'Well, damn it, as far as I can gather, there was a company holding the mining lease years back which could have done the job just as well, and without selling ourselves off to American capital, either! It's just that Streisman, like the bloody entrepreneurial pirate he is, saw some opportunities and stepped in to buy up options and leases to make his own company kingpin. But there's a lot of people don't like it, you know. Down here in Devon, well, we're not as bad as the Cornish, but we like to feel we have our own identity, you know? And there's a lot of resentment arising against the operation at Ottershaw.'

'I've seen some of it,' Crow observed.

Carr raised his eyebrows. 'The fuss they're making in the village itself? Oh yes, we know about that. The way I hear it, though, it's only the start. They got a group there who are starting to tap other sources, and there's talk of the Bristol Activists people coming in to lend some muscle.'

'So I understand.'

'It's something you'd be well out of,' Carr suggested. 'You know Streisman has put in a request for a police guard at Ottershaw when the pilot plant is opened?'

'I assume that's because the Minister will be present.'

'And Streisman himself,' Carr sneered. 'This is one time he won't be getting what he wants, nevertheless: we got a royal visit up here, and that means top security, so all the county strength is going to be concentrated in the area of the city. If we can spare anything at all for the plant opening, it'll be a token force — and Streisman can offer as much by way of payment as he likes — it'll do him no good.'

Crow got the impression that Carr was not displeased at the thought of Streisman being put in his place by royalty: it would serve to show him money could not buy everything. 'Still, to get back to the Norman situation,' Crow said, 'I've got hold of his work diary, and a notebook from his cottage—'

'How the hell did we miss those?' Carr rumbled, frowning.

'Well, no matter, it was probably before you got on the case,' Crow said, mollifying him, 'but the main thing is, did you get around to working out what Norman was up to in the last weeks before his death?'

Carr clenched his pipe with his back teeth, leaned back in his chair and folded his arms. 'Aye, did that all right. If you take a look in that folder right there — second from the top — you'll see the breakdown I compiled myself. Shortly after I did that I was taken off the case, pending your arrival. But Norman's movements — with dates they're all there, as far as I could manage.'

Crow took out the file and inspected the contents. Carr waited, smoking quietly, while Crow went through the details.

'Mmm. It checks out with his diary entries, anyway,' Crow remarked. 'Let's see. If we go back to . . . what . . . January 20, he paid a visit to Brigadier Leveson. Fine . . . now for several days he was working on site, then there was a week's leave. Right, now on January 25 he paid another visit to the Brigadier. That would be when he had a disagreement with Leveson over the contractual arrangements.'

'I wouldn't know about that,' Carr said.

'The Brigadier told Delaval the discussion took place some six or eight weeks before Norman died.' Crow paused, frowning, then shook his head in annoyance as the thought that had fluttered into his mind stubbornly refused to take shape once more. 'Now then, on February 5 Norman came up to Exeter. As far as records show, there was no company meeting at the Exeter headquarters, nor did he call in there. Do you have any idea what he was doing in the city that day?'

Carr shook his head. 'I did begin to make enquiries, but they were as fruitless as they were short-lived.'

Crow nodded. He checked the diary against the file prepared by Carr; both agreed that Fred Norman had spent a few days back on the site again thereafter until February 8. 'This is where he started his tour of the garages that serviced Streisman vehicles. It went on until the 12th of the month. You know what connection that was, do you?'

Carr removed his pipe and inspected its bowl. He tamped the tobacco gingerly with his finger. 'He was doing another check over that Ottershaw road accident. He'll have come up with nothing. When I saw that entry, I checked our own files. We made enquiries at local garages; no Streisman lorry was involved in that death.'

'No trace of the hit-and-run driver since?'

Carr shrugged. 'Not my department. But I gather not.

'This Fred Norman, though — he was a conscientious chap, wasn't he? I mean, all right, he's the Environmental Coordinator, but he doesn't half juggle a few balls in the air at the same time. And delving like that was a big job. At the same time he's trying to sweeten Leveson, monitor the programmes running on site, dashing up to Exeter, arguing the toss with that village action group — committed, frenetic, call it what you will, but he certainly had energy.'

Crow mused for a little while, then asked, 'What other views do you have of Norman?'

'Shadowy,' Carr admitted. 'A loner; quiet; maybe introverted. But one of a type.'

'How do you mean?'

Carr looked vaguely surprised. 'Well, they're all the same, don't you notice? To start with, they're all as good as being bloody bachelors—'

'That, I gather, is a Myron Streisman policy,' Crow said drily. 'He seems to think he gets more commitment out of his senior men that way.'

'Okay, but they're all loners, too, didn't you see?' He relit his pipe and puffed hard at it. 'They don't mix much with each other. You'd expect maybe one or two of them would be friends, with interests in common, but that isn't so. The nearest to a human being is Fairfield — he at least lives in the village and knows the locals; but the others, they not only don't know each other too well, they don't seem to have put down any roots anywhere in the county, even after two, three years. How the hell they can pull together on the project I don't know. Maybe they don't.'

It was a point Crow had not considered or noted, but he felt it was a valuable one. He was pleased he had asked Carr to talk with him about the case. 'After the garage check,' he went on, 'Norman would seem to have visited the Brigadier again.'

'Ahuh. I don't know why, though.'

'Nor do I. Inspector Delaval's report states that Leveson told him the last meeting was the one in January.'

'A mistake?'

'Maybe. Anyway . . . and that about ends what we know of Norman's movements. A visit to Brigadier Leveson on the 17th; work on site, it seems thereafter, until he was found dead on the morning of the 20th, after being missed the previous day.'

After a short silence, Carr said, 'I guess you're in no position yet, either, to start contemplating motives.'

Crow shook his head. 'It's perhaps the only thing I *am* certain of in this case: I've no idea *why* Fred Norman was murdered.'

* * *

It was mid-afternoon before Delaval joined Crow at headquarters. He had spent several hours at the Exeter main office of the Streisman Corporation, and had gone through the details of the agreements reached by Leveson's uncle with the company, the resultant disagreements with Leveson himself, the court proceedings that had been instituted and the papers relating to the planning enquiries.

'To be quite honest,' Delaval said, pushing back the usual errant lock of fair hair from his eyes, 'I'm at a bit of a loss to work out what Leveson is playing at. No doubt he's got cash in the bank, and pride, but he's throwing money away, It seems to me. I just don't see how he'll win over the options thing. At best, he's only getting rid of some spite, in delaying the company. But what's the point of that?'

'Leveson . . .' Crow leaned forward, angular chin resting on one hand, elbow on the desk. 'Leveson . . . You reported he said the last time he saw Norman was six or eight weeks ago?'

'Right.'

'Norman's diary suggests they met again, on February 17, Just days before he died.'

Delaval shook his head. 'Leveson didn't mention that.'

'And what did they talk about at the meeting he admits *did* take place?'

'They had a row — about what Leveson saw as an attempt to get out of the royalties arrangement he'd negotiated with Norman.'

'Curious.' It was there again in the back of Crow's mind, hovering, formless but insistent. Something he had missed; something important. He reached into the desk drawer, took out the report Fred Norman had prepared for Pete Harris and gazed at it thoughtfully. He looked up at Delaval, frowning. 'I want you to get this report up to the forensic laboratories at Bristol, as soon as possible. A rush job; you can tell them that.'

'What'll they be looking for?' Delaval asked.

'I don't know. But I've got a . . . feeling about it.' When he caught Delaval's grin, Crow smiled himself. 'We're all entitled to hunches from time to time. And I've got one about this.'

'While I've got an odd one about Brigadier Leveson,' Delaval said, laughing.

'Then chase it up. What's good for the old goose should be good for the young one. But get mine sorted out first: seniority.'

'I'll do that, sir.' As Delaval rose with the report in his hand, the telephone rang, and with an exaggerated care the detective inspector picked up the phone and intoned, 'Detective Superintendent Crow's office.'

Crow smiled and waited. Delaval stood stiffly to attention for a few seconds, then shot a quick glance at Crow, raised his eyebrows, put down the report and sat down again. He listened without speaking for almost a minute, and then, finally, nodded, thanked the speaker at the other end of the phone and replaced the phone on its cradle.

'Bristol,' he said.

Crow raised his eyebrows. 'Jack Prince?'

'That's right, sir. I asked them to run a check on Prince's alibi for the night Norman was murdered. It looks now as though we might not need to pursue our . . . er . . . hunches. Jack Prince's alibi . . . it just won't hold water.'

CHAPTER 4

Delaval and Crow left the car near the Miner's Arms and climbed the hill to Portworthy Cottages together. In the early evening a haze had settled over the moors above Ottershaw, blurring the outlines of the spoil-heaps, and darkening the pale blue evening sky. The air was still, carrying with a sharp clarity the rumbling of traffic through the village, the sound of children playing in a garden at the foot of the hill, the barking of a dog. In one of the grey stone cottages an altercation between a man and a woman, shrill, obscene in the language used, shattered the quiet of the hill; two doors away from Marlene Park's house a child sat on the front step, watching the two policemen with a bored indifference. Delaval smiled at the boy, but there was no response. Crow knocked at Marlene Park's door.

He was forced to knock three times before the door finally opened. Jack Prince stood there; he wore no shirt, and the string vest that covered his upper body had seen better days, while the stained knees of his baggy, sagging trousers suggested that he might have been working in the small garden at the back of the cottage when Crow knocked. He expressed surprise at seeing the two policemen, but there was something else in his eyes apart from surprise. He was edgy and nervous, and he darted quick glances behind them, down the hill.

'Marlene's not in at the moment,' he explained. 'She had some shopping to do, and then she said she'd be calling in to see someone. I'm not expecting her back for maybe half an hour or so.'

'We didn't really come to see her,' Crow said. 'Wanted to have a chat with you. Er . . . it would be better, maybe, if we went inside.'

Prince was reluctant to extend the invitation. He looked across the line of the cottages and caught the eye of the boy sitting in the doorway. The child poked out his tongue, and Prince muttered something under his breath. 'Brat,' he said. 'They're all brats here on the hill. All right, you'd better come inside. Mind if I go and have a wash first?'

He led the way along a short passage and gestured them to take seats in the small sitting-room that led off on the left. He walked through the kitchen to the extension at the back of the cottage where, apparently, the bathroom was located. Crow guessed the cottages must have had bathrooms built on under the development grants of recent years; upstairs there would be room only for two bedrooms. He looked around at the sitting-room: a three-piece suite with worn arms, an expensive stereogram, cheap imitation panelling on one wall, and a mass-produced picture of a Spanish dancer on another. No books, no magazines, but copies of two tabloid newspapers. On the mantelpiece a photograph of a young girl.

Delaval picked it up, and studied it. 'I guess this will be the daughter who was killed.'

Crow looked at it. It was a studio photograph which must have been taken perhaps a year before she died. A round face, direct eyes that carried a hint of the boldness that was apparent in the eyes of her mother. Dark hair, cut short; she looked older than Crow had expected — he would have put her at perhaps seventeen or eighteen, but she had only been fifteen when the vehicle had killed her in the main street of Ottershaw.

'That's Freda.' Prince had come into the room, towel in hand, shirt on but unbuttoned as he dried his hands.

'We thought it probably was,' Crow replied. He waited as Prince buttoned his shirt and tossed the damp towel over the radiator behind the door. 'Can we talk now?'

'Lemme get a beer first.' It was as though Prince was reluctant that the interview should begin; at the same time he was plainly nervous they might be interrupted, for he glanced at his watch and looked out of the front window down the hill towards the village. 'I been working out the back, laying some slabs: thirsty work. You . . . er . . . you want a drink?' When Crow and Delaval both refused, Prince went back into the kitchen, where they heard him open the refrigerator. He came back into the room with a can of beer and, having opened it, began to drink directly from the can.

'We've called,' Crow explained, 'to ask you a few more questions about Fred Norman.'

'Fire away.'

'The quarrel you had with him — was it the only one?'

Prince raised his shoulders. 'We had words several times over the street issue. But that was the only time we had a go at each other in public, if you know what I mean. In the committee, and once or twice up at the site when I went up there to see him, we had a few words, but quarrels . . . no, just the once.'

'You visited him at the site?' Delaval asked. 'You know the pilot plant area fairly well, then?'

Jack Prince's eyes flickered from Crow to Delaval. 'I did a spell as a dumper driver on the site right at the beginning. Just for six weeks. I wouldn't say I know the site well — but why do you ask, anyway?' He licked his lips. 'If you're trying to suggest—'

'We're suggesting nothing yet,' Crow interrupted. 'The quarrel you had with Norman was, as you explained, specifically concerned with the road issue. Did you have any other bones of contention with him?'

Prince shook his head. 'Naw. Had nothin' else to do with him, in fact.' He took a long drink from his beer can and then squinted across at Crow. 'You can't make nothin' out of that quarrel, you know. All right, I lost my temper, but so did he, and people don't go around killing people just because they had words.'

'In any case,' Crow said mildly, 'you weren't even in the area when Norman died, were you?'

Prince's glance froze. After a few moments he nodded. 'That's right.'

'You went to Bristol, to see the Activists. Can you give us precise details, Mr Prince?'

'No sweat. Marlene drove me into Plymouth in the morning; I got a train about eleven, I think it was. I was with these people I went to see all afternoon, and I didn't feel like rushin' back down here that evening, so I went out and had a few drinks in a pub I know down by the quayside. Next morning I took the train back to Plymouth, and got a bus out to the village here.'

'Where did you stay that evening?' Delaval asked. Prince's glance was evasive. 'I . . . I can't remember the name of the place. It was a small guesthouse in one of the roads up behind the Victoria Rooms. Had a bit of trouble, I did, finding a place. Bloody awful breakfast, too. The eggs wasn't cooked, even.'

Crow was unimpressed by the detail added to convince; he smiled faintly at Prince and said, 'I think it would be useful if you were to make a formal statement along those lines. Just so we're sure we know exactly what you're saying.'

Alarm was registered in Prince's face, and he put down his can of beer, glancing from one policeman to the other. 'Statement? What the hell are you talking about?'

'Well, we'd find a statement useful if we are to make a formal check of your movements at that time.'

'*Formal* check?'

'That's right. You see, as a matter of course we would naturally make some enquiries to back up what you've told us so far. Not a detailed, formal check on your movements — in the first instance, merely a telephone call to the Bristol CID to ask them if they'd oblige us by making an initial check.'

'And that's what we did,' Delaval went on. 'The trouble is, Mr Prince, you didn't take the trouble to lay the groundwork for your . . . ah . . . alibi very soundly. I got a phone call today from Bristol: they'd interviewed the gentleman you'd met from the Activists group up there, and *his* story differs significantly from yours.'

'I don't see—'

'*He* reckons,' Delaval continued, 'that the meeting was over by four in the afternoon, and that since there was a train leaving within half an hour you decided to catch it back to Plymouth. Moreover, he told the Bristol police that he actually drove you to Templemeads in order to catch that train.'

'I didn't get it! I missed it!' Prince's tone was urgent. 'I missed it, so decided to stay on.'

There was a short silence. 'You missed it,' Crow said flatly. 'And then walked back across the city, from the station, to find accommodation?'

'That's right.'

'And then came back across the city again, to drink near the quayside? Wouldn't it have been simpler to get a guesthouse near Templemeads?'

Prince shrugged. 'Didn't think about it.'

'But you stayed near the Victoria Rooms — and you can't tell us where. No matter. If you'll give us what details you can remember now, we'll get a formal check made at Bristol to verify your story.'

'What the hell's this about?' Prince rose to his feet and began to prowl around the room. 'You trying to tie me in with Norman's murder? I'm not going to have — oh, hell's bells!'

He had stopped just in front of the window. Crow could see past him, down the hill, and he too saw the car that was being driven up towards the cottages. It was the vehicle he had seen parked in the main street a few days ago, at the time of the altercation with the lorry-driver. It was Marlene Park's car.

Prince swung around to face the two policemen. 'Look, Marlene's coming back. I don't want her worried . . . or involved in this. I'd prefer if . . . if we could talk about this later—'

'I'm afraid that won't do,' Crow said coldly. 'You've given us a story that doesn't hold water and we need to have an early explanation, or more details which will enable us to corroborate your movements on the night Norman died.'

'But you can't think I had anything to do with that killing!'

'We're not saying you did, but this discrepancy—'

'All right, all right, oh hell, Marlene'll be here in a few minutes . . . Look, if you'll come out through the back we can walk along the lane there, and I can explain out there. But if Marlene comes in she'll want to know what this is all about and there'll be all hell to pay. Please — can we go out through the back?'

The air of belligerence had gone, and Crow's suspicion that Marlene Park was the more dominant partner in the relationship was confirmed. He nodded, gestured to Delaval. 'All right, we'll do as you ask.'

Gratefully Prince hurried ahead of them through the kitchen towards the back of the house. They heard the car stop at the front of the house; Delaval grinned at Crow as they walked out behind Prince into the lane there was an element of farce in the proceedings that amused him. Crow regarded the situation more seriously.

'All right,' he said coldly to Prince. 'Let's talk.'

The lane was narrow and stony, lying under the rise of the hill, between the backs of the houses in the terrace and a supporting stone wall built against the rising ground. Prince shoved his hands in his pockets and shivered slightly. 'Can we move just along a way? She'll be able to see us from the kitchen, otherwise . . .' He shook his head angrily. 'All right, there's no need to take a statement, and no need to do any more checking. Fact is, I wasn't in Bristol that night.'

'You came back here to Ottershaw?' Delaval asked.

Prince nodded. 'That's right. I caught the train all right. But you see . . . Look, I'd better tell you the whole story. I been living with Marlene for a couple of years now, but, well, that doesn't mean a man's got to stay away from other women, if you know what I mean. Just because I live with her it doesn't mean she bloody well owns me.' His defiance was ill-placed, since he was confronting the two policemen, not Marlene Park, but he injected more belligerence into his tone. 'The way she goes on you'd think she *did* bloody own me, for all that! But I see no reason . . . Anyway, the fact is I came back to Ottershaw that night all right, but I didn't come back up here to Portworthy Cottages. I stayed somewhere else, and . . . and with someone else, not Marlene.'

'Who were you with?' Crow asked.

'I don't see why you got to know that!' Prince flared. 'I'm telling you the truth. I was here but—'

'Mr Prince. You had a quarrel with Fred Norman shortly before he died. You gave us a false story of your whereabouts at the crucial time. You now tell us another story. We'll have to corroborate it by speaking to the person concerned.'

'Now look—'

'The name, Mr Prince,' Crow said firmly.

Jack Prince was silent. He stared at the ground, most of his toughness dissipated, an anxious and worried man. He kicked at a stone with his shoe, then shook his head.

'What a bloody mess . . . She's called Morgan. Ginny Morgan.'

'Where does she live?' Delaval asked.

'The smallholding — at the far end of the village. But . . . will you have to talk to her?'

'We will,' Crow confirmed.

'She could lie,' Prince said with a hint of desperation. 'She could swear I was never there.'

'She could,' Crow admitted. 'But why would she do so?'

'She's only just sixteen,' Jack Prince said miserably. Delaval glanced at Crow and raised his eyebrows. The two policemen were silent for a few moments and then Crow asked, 'And how long have you been sleeping with her?'

Prince gritted his teeth, grinding them. 'There've been a few times, over the last year. But she might lie about it.'

'She's not *committed* to you, then?' Delaval asked.

Prince groaned. 'Oh, for God's sake, get it straight right now! Commitment? Look, she's been offering herself around for two years and more, to my knowledge! She lives with her father, who couldn't give a damn as long as she doesn't bother him too much, and he was up at Holsworthy that night, so I arranged with her to come back and spend the night. All right, I'd been with her before, but I was itching for her again, so I fixed it up. I stayed at her place that night, but her father wouldn't have known about it, and no one saw me, I was out by dawn and down to Plymouth on the early bus. But commitment? She's a little madam, that one, a real bad one. She's been after me for long enough, but just for the hell of it. And just for the hell of it now, she's likely to lie in her teeth and say I was never there.'

'How did you come to start this . . . liaison?' Crow asked.

'Ah, it started some time back. Ginny, she was a bit older of course, but she was friendly with Freda, Marlene's daughter.' He grimaced. 'In some ways they was two of a kind. She used to come up to the cottages and sit around upstairs playing records, lying around, and when I was here and Marlene wasn't around the little bitch used to give me the eye, lead me on, you know? Then one day when Marlene had taken Freda into Plymouth Ginny came around, pretending she wanted to see Freda. But what she really wanted . . . well, she got it.'

'And at that time she would be . . . fifteen?'

Prince made no reply. Crow glanced at Delaval. He could guess what the inspector would be thinking. It would be unlikely that Prince would make up such a story, putting himself at risk of facing a criminal charge for having sexual relations with a girl under the age of consent. But Crow was not so sure. If Ginny Morgan denied Prince's story, it would not necessarily mean she was lying — whether or not Prince had been her lover on other occasions. He frowned. 'You said she was a friend of Freda Park's, and that the two girls were . . . alike?'

Prince made a gesture of impatience. 'I don't mean that Freda was sleeping around the way Ginny's been since God knows when. Precocious little bugger . . . No, but Freda was . . . influenced by Ginny. You know, she thought it was clever to dress older than she really was, look older, use make-up, talk clever, being obvious with men, you know. I told her once or twice she ought to stop playing up to blokes the way she did, it'd get her into trouble.'

'You told her this,' Delaval said wonderingly, 'at the same time that you were sleeping with her friend?'

'Just because I was doing that,' Prince said angrily, 'it didn't mean I shouldn't give Freda the kind of warning her father would have given her if he'd been around!'

'All right,' Crow nodded, 'never mind about that. We're concerned about your whereabouts on the night in question, not the behaviour of Ginny Morgan and Freda Park. Mr Prince, if that's all you have to tell us we'll leave it there for now. But we'll have to check your story with Ginny Morgan.'

Prince's eyes glowed maliciously. 'She'll lie,' he said, with venom in his tone. 'I know she'll bloody well lie!'

* * *

Late the following afternoon Delaval joined John Crow in his office. Over a cup of tea he reported his interview with the sixteen-year-old Virginia Morgan. She was, it seemed, rather more mature a personality than her sixteen years would lead one to expect. She looked twenty, had a figure that could be described as voluptuous, and when angry was able to display a command of the English vernacular that testified without doubt to the kind of company she was in the habit of keeping. In Delaval's opinion it was possible that she might have been seduced when she was fourteen or so, but he doubted it; rather, it would have been Virginia Morgan who had done the seducing. Nor had that first experience put her off men for life; on the contrary, she had developed what would seem to be a somewhat voracious appetite for the aggregation of new experiences.

'You mean she tried to seduce *you?'* Crow said in surprise.

'Don't make it sound such an inexplicable desire on her part,' Delaval protested. 'Women have been known to fancy me.'

'Sixteen-year-olds?'

'I have explained — Ginny can be described as anything but a sixteen-year-old, apart from her chronological age!'

And Jack Prince had been right about one thing: the girl in question was determined to deny that he had spent the night with her when Fred Norman died. Delaval was not able to be confident she was lying: she did not deny the fact of an affair — 'off and on', as she put it — with Prince, but she would not admit that he had been with her on the night in question in her own bedroom. Delaval was prepared to try to explain *why* she might be lying, if she was.

'She's a girl who likes to create sensations, but feels cheated if the sensation is not of her own making. If *she* had told me that a thirty-year-old man, Jack Prince, had slept with her while her father was up at Holsworthy, that would have been one thing: she would have been hoping to shock me, or at the very least, *interest* me. But my knowing about it, because I'd been told by Prince himself, that was different — such revelations were her prerogative, and Jack Prince hadn't played her game by telling me. So her reaction is to deny it.'

'So she *is* lying?' Crow asked.

'I can't be certain of that. But if she is that'll be the reason.'

'That does not,' Crow commented, 'get us very far. We need corroboration of the situation — and unfortunately, acts of that kind are rarely completed in public.'

Delaval still held the opinion that it was unlikely Prince was telling lies, since it put him at risk of prosecution. Crow countered by pointing out that a charge of criminal assault was better than a charge of murder, particularly in view of the difficulties inherent in proving the former charge if Ginny Morgan should later change her mind about admitting sexual acts with Jack Prince.

'And she might even do that,' Delaval admitted. 'She's got some curiously ambivalent views about Prince. I got the feeling she had deliberately seduced him, a year or so back, because she knew he was having lecherous thoughts about the daughter of his mistress.'

'You can't be serious!'

'It's the impression I got. Ginny Morgan was the older girl, and the one who was bringing Freda Park out of her youthful innocence, but there was a hint of jealousy in some of the remarks she made to me about Freda Park. I suspect she found that not only was Freda learning faster than she might have expected, but she was capable of being more obvious in her attitudes towards boys than even Ginny was.'

'Prince certainly saw them as birds of a feather,' Crow admitted.

'And flocking into the same nest,' Delaval agreed, 'at Marlene Park's house. I get the impression Freda started to use Prince — a male stranger in her mother's house — as a sexual sounding-board, maybe without knowing too much what she was doing at first, and then little Ginny stepped in to get there first.'

'She didn't tell you Prince slept with Freda Park!'

'No, no,' Delaval said, 'in fact she said she was pretty sure Freda never knew any man, and was still virginal when she was knocked down. But she also hinted it wasn't for want of trying . . . or to put it another way, if she was still a virgin, it wasn't because she'd fought shy of sex.'

'How do you mean?'

Delaval explained that apparently the two girls had tended to wander through the village during the evenings, flirting and talking with boys — and sometimes teasing men who were leaving the Miner's Arms. Most of the locals had taken it in good part and regarded it as nonsense, though there had been the occasional lorry-driver who had become pressing in his responses to their teasing, at which Ginny and Freda had fled the scene, giggling.

'The sexual life of the typical Devon village,' Crow said in mock wonderment. 'All very interesting, sociologically speaking, but it gets us no further.'

'As you say, sir. It leaves us with the fact that at the moment, our friend Prince can't *prove* he was with Ginny Morgan that night—'

'And he *had* quarrelled with Fred Norman—'

'But every time I see him, and the longer I talk with him,' Delaval demurred, 'the weaker a character he seems to be.'

'In his relationships with women, yes,' Crow agreed. 'He can't handle Marlene Park, that's for sure. But he *has* lied to us, and among men, well, if he was drunk enough and angry enough, I still think he could have crushed the back of Fred Norman's skull.'

'Was his motive strong enough?'

'That maybe remains to be seen. We must certainly keep an eye on him. But,' Crow added, 'there's something else turned up now which is going to engage my attention rather more closely. I've just had a letter from Bristol, from the forensic laboratories. You'd better read it.'

The letter was brief and to the point. Delaval read it quickly.

For the attention of Detective Superintendent Crow. The enclosed report, the property of Streisman Corporation, was received under urgent cover for analysis yesterday. No instructions were received regarding the enquiries which were to be raised in regard to the report, so a complete check was carried out on the whole document. No attempt has been made to verify the scientific and engineering data it contains, this being outside the scope and expertise of staff at these laboratories. Detailed investigation of the document otherwise discloses little of interest, though the appended statements highlight the nature of the paper used, the type of machine used for typing, the variance in typing skills, the biological nature of certain stains on some of the sheets, etc.'

Delaval looked up to John Crow. 'What were the stains?' he asked.

'Coffee,' Crow stated drily. 'Read on.'

'The only particular point which seems worthy of note regarding the report, therefore, would seem to be its dating. The use of infra-red spectroscopy would seem to suggest that not only has the original date of the report been changed, but that a deliberate attempt has been made to hide the fact of the change. The details are again referred to in the schedule to this letter, but briefly, it may be confidently reported that the original date has been eradicated by methods noted in the schedule, that a new date was substituted, and that the relevant sheets were then photocopied with the new date, to increase their likely veracity and minimize the possibility of the change being discovered.'

Crow smiled coldly as Delaval looked up. 'In other words,' he said, 'it wasn't just a straightforward change of date — eradication and overtyping would have sorted that out. Instead, they report a deliberate attempt to mislead. Difficult to prove, but they include the details in the schedule, and those boys in Bristol are prepared to put it in writing that it does amount to an attempt to mislead.'

'An attempt by whom?' Delaval asked.

'That's what I mean to find out,' Crow said. 'By whom, and why? But that's my pigeon. As for Jack Prince, let him simmer for another day or so. Have you finished your check on Norman's visit to Exeter, yet?'

'Another day, two at the most.'

'Then you get on with that. Me, it's back to the Ottershaw site, I'm afraid, for another chat to the senior management team of the Streisman Corporation.'

* * *

It was raining the following day. It came down in long, slanting sheets, driving down from the hills, cloaking the moor in thick mists, and causing rivulets to run across the site towards the trenches beyond the old workings of the mine. Lorries entering the site sent up bow-waves of spray as they surged through a wide pool that had formed just inside the main gate, and when John Crow drove on to the site and stopped to wind down his window and identify himself to the gateman, his shirt collar was quickly dampened as needle-points of cold, driving rain forced their way against his face and neck.

Having been waved through, he parked as near as possible to Ray Grainger's office, and then made a long-legged dash to reach the office before he was soaked by the rain. As he entered, hatless, water streaming down over his bald head and gaunt features, he knew he would look a sight: Janet stared at him in some embarrassment until he smiled and said, 'A cup of coffee would be very welcome.'

'I'll make you one straight away,' she said. 'Mr Grainger's alone. I'll tell him you're here.'

Grainger, too, it seemed, would find a cup of coffee welcome, and he pushed his papers aside to talk to Crow while they waited for Janet to return.

'How is the investigation proceeding?' he asked.

'Slowly. And how are the arrangements for the plant opening coming along?' Crow countered.

Grainger grimaced. 'You might have heard the police are being a bit uncooperative. There'll be a token force here, apparently — not that we're likely to have problems of crowd control—'

'Unless there's a demonstration,' Crow interrupted. That's just hot air.' Grainger's gesture was dismissive, and he seemed to discount even the possibility of such activity on the site.

'We could stop them at the gateway, in any case. The Minister and Mr Streisman will be arriving by helicopter and staying just an hour — a quick tour of the site, two short speeches, and then a Press Conference, which I'll be handling.'

'Won't Streisman want to do that?'

Grainger smiled warily. 'Normally, perhaps, but I gather he and Foster will be going on to another meeting in Plymouth. Financial aid from the Government, so it's important enough to override a Press Conference here on site.'

'Mmmm.' Crow paused while Janet came in with two coffees. When she had left again, he turned back to Grainger. 'I've been checking on what Norman was up to during the last weeks before his death, and Janet told me he was working on some kind of report. Do *you* know what it was?'

Grainger shook his head. 'Not off-hand. We . . . well, we've tended to work towards our own responsibilities—'

'But you're Project Manager. I would have thought you'd be the one with an overall view.'

Grainger's cheeks grew pink at the implied criticism. 'That's so, but when you have qualified men working with you, delegation is sensible — and in our case, necessary. As for Norman's report, he was working on a number of issues — it could have been in respect of any of them. If anyone is likely to know what Fred was working on though, it would be Pete Harris. He spent a fair bit of time with Fred recently, since the explorations side obviously had most impact on the problems Fred had to handle.'

'I've spoken to Harris. He wasn't able to help much. He did give me this report, however. Have you seen it?'

Crow handed the report folder to Grainger, who opened it, read some of the data and then closed it again. He sat staring at it for a few minutes, thinking. Then he nodded. 'Yes, I've seen it. There's probably a copy in my files.'

'May I see it?'

Grainger looked up, surprise in his eyes. 'Of course. I'll call Janet.' He spoke to the secretary over the intercom and asked her to raise the report for him; then he leaned back, smiling quizzically. 'This a test of our filing systems, Superintendent?'

Crow made no reply. He waited until Janet brought in Grainger's copy of the report, and then looked at it briefly. It held the same date as that on the one in Crow's possession.

'Any problem?' Grainger asked.

'None.' Crow finished his coffee. 'I think I'd better brave the rain again, and get across to see Mr Harris.'

'You're sure there's no problem?' Grainger asked, and Crow stared at him. There had been an edge of nervous uncertainty in the man's tone, and Crow waited, letting whatever pressures were affecting the man build up inside him. 'I . . . I just wondered,' Grainger faltered, 'whether it was anything to do with the figures and data Norman had written in his notebook.'

'Why? Have you had further thoughts about them?'

'Me? Oh no . . . some of them were wrong, that's all, but I've not bothered further about them.'

Ray Grainger had lowered his eyelids, as though seeking to hide his emotions from John Crow, but the injection of earnest honesty into his voice brought back to Crow the remarks Delaval had first made about the Project Manager. Now, he had the impression that Grainger was backing away from him mentally; the man was afraid he had exposed something in his nervousness, and wished to draw back from the edge of the precipice suddenly yawning in front of him. Crow hesitated: he could pursue it now, or let the man's questions die away, indecisively, inside him, until Crow himself had more information with which to rattle him.

For Grainger was nervous and more; fear brought a light sheen of perspiration to his upper lip. Crow would want to know what had caused that fear.

Outside, the rain had become torrential in its ferocity.

Crow made his way to Pete Harris's office, the rain forcing its way under the collar of his raincoat and dripping down his neck. He found Harris in his office with Alan Fairfield. Fairfield looked up as Crow knocked and entered, and said he'd be leaving in a moment.

'I hear you've been to see Jack Prince again,' he said.

'News travels fast,' Crow said, raising his eyebrows in surprise.

Fairfield shrugged. 'Small village: not much happening — so the talk in the pub is mainly of your investigations into Fred Norman's death, naturally, and if you pay a couple of visits to see Jack Prince, well, local tongues start wagging. Did . . . er . . . did anything transpire?'

'Would you expect me to tell you?' Crow said, smiling faintly.

Alan Fairfield grinned. 'No, I reckon not. Anyway, I'll get out of your way.' He hesitated, glancing uncertainly at Pete Harris, seemed to be about to add something, and then thought better of it. He nodded to Crow and left. Pete Harris sat up straighter in his chair.

'Well, Superintendent?'

'A few questions, Mr Harris.'

'Again?' Harris seemed somewhat nettled, annoyed that he was being disturbed once more by John Crow. But his eyes had fastened on the report that he had given to Crow, and which the policeman had now taken out from under his raincoat. Crow placed it on the desk between them, took off his coat and sat down. Harris tried to look away from the document, but his glance returned to it several times, nervously.

'I've been through this report of Fred Norman's,' Crow said quietly. 'As you said, it's concerned with the ore body, and the equipment and so on. The curious thing is, it mentions nothing about drilling arrangements and details.'

Pete Hams licked his lips and managed to look puzzled. 'There's no reason why it should. It was a study that—'

'But my conversation with Janet led me to believe that Mr Norman had been concerning himself with drilling operations, and that he had been discussing them with you.'

There was a short silence. 'I think Janet must be . . . wrong. Or forgetful. I don't know what she might have been talking about.'

John Crow looked at his notebook. 'Odd ...You remember the notebook Norman had left at his house? It contained some data on drilling figures.'

'Which were wrong.'

Crow nodded. 'That's right. He didn't discuss *those* with you?'

Harris shook his head. 'I told you—'

'Nor the other information in his notebook?' When Harris again shook his head, Crow frowned. 'And this report you gave me . . . it's dated February 16. I find that somewhat . . . strange.'

Harris hesitated. His glance flickered once more to the report. 'Strange? Why?'

'Ray Grainger has a copy of this report.'

'So?'

'Well, it's the sequence of events that I find strange.' Crow tapped the report of Fred Norman with a long, predatory finger. 'You see, Fred Norman's diary shows what he was doing, generally speaking, during the last few months. And on January 25 he visited Brigadier Leveson. It wasn't a very . . . ah . . . amicable meeting.'

'I wouldn't know—'

'Please, let me finish,' Crow admonished, holding up a bony hand. 'Norman had been negotiating with Leveson for some time — it concerned the payment of royalties for any wolframite mined over the tongue of land adjacent to this site and owned by Leveson. Now, on January 25 Leveson *summoned* Norman to his house because he had heard rumours regarding certain land purchases to the west of this site. Can you tell me when those purchases were taken up?'

Harris frowned; his fingers stole nervously up to his mouth. He shook his head. 'Not for certain.'

'Roughly, then? Last December? January? February?'

'I believe,' Harris said stiffly, 'the options to purchase were taken up at the end of January.'

'Which would account for Leveson hearing about it, around about the 25th. A man of his kind would have contacts among land agents . . . Yes, I see. Now, when he saw Norman they quarrelled because Leveson had realized, or had heard, that the mining operations would not, in fact, give rise to any royalties payable to him because mining would not be carried out on the tongue of land owned by him. He regarded that as sharp practice. When Delaval told me this, I was surprised — for Myron Streisman prides himself on being a straight businessman. It could have been an occasion when Homer nodded, of course . . . but now I have rather a different view of it.'

Harris licked his lips again. His voice was husky. 'View of what?'

'Of the discussion between the Brigadier and Fred Norman. There was no question of sharp practice being involved, whatever Leveson thought about it. There was a perfectly good reason why the land was bought; there was a sound reason why the mining would not be carried on over that tongue of land. You gave me that reason last time we spoke.'

'I—'

'You told me the shape of the mining operation on an open-cast base, though normally undertaken as a series of concentric circles, was actually determined by the shape of the ore body.'

'That's precisely the situation. But I don't see where this is getting us,' Harris said irritably. 'I have a great deal of work to do and—'

'I'll tell you where it's leading me, Mr Harris,' Crow said sharply. 'It leads me to the conclusion that the decision to change the shape of the mining operation had been taken before the end of January, and that consequently land purchase options were being taken up. Leveson heard about it and had a confrontation with Fred Norman — who already knew the situation regarding the ore body. So what I can't understand is this. *Why should Norman put that report to you on February 16?'*

'Because that's when he completed it,' Harris said testily.

'I find that difficult to understand. The report makes specific recommendations on equipment that would be environmentally suitable — based on knowledge regarding the ore body shape. This wasn't done until February?'

'I see no reason—'

'I would have thought that data and those recommendations would have been at the least contemporary with the land option purchases! I would have thought a report of this kind may well have preceded such decisions. I would certainly have thought Norman would have had this information for some time before he saw Leveson on the 25th!'

'I can't vouch for what information he had or didn't have at that time. Really, Superintendent—'

Crow held up a warning hand. 'One moment, Mr Harris. I'll ask you again. This report was given to you?' When Harris nodded, Crow asked, 'And you gave the report to Grainger in February?'

'Late February, early March.'

'Do you normally give interim reports of this kind to him?'

Harris shrugged. 'Not always. He . . . he believes in delegation, and doesn't concern himself with details.'

'But you had to put this one in to him, didn't you?' Crow smiled thinly. 'I mean, it covered you, didn't it, in the event of questions being asked?'

The silence grew around them. Pete Harris had paled; his eyes had become glazed, and he hardly appeared to be able to focus on Crow. 'What . . . what do you mean by that remark?' he asked huskily.

'I had a curious . . . feeling about this report. I put it into the labs for a forensic check. And after the check I looked more closely at the detail. I'm led to the conclusion that this report was not written in February, but weeks, maybe months earlier.'

'You can't prove—'

'The date has been changed. The forensic boys tell me the change was made deliberately, in their view. I asked myself why. And I looked at the details. Fred Norman knew these facts, and wrote this report — *and dated it* much earlier. *You* had it on file; you changed the date; photocopied the original; put it back on file and sent a copy to Grainger so he too had it on file.'

'Why the hell should I do that?' Harris burst out.

'Because, if the question were asked — what was Fred Norman working on before he died? — you could produce an answer. This report.'

'That's a lot of nonsense, and there's no way—'

'So what *was* he working on, Harris?' Crow interrupted, with iron in his voice. 'Between the end of January and February 8 there's a blank — he was working on something, which he completed before he started another check on the garages in the area because of pressure brought over the Ottershaw accident months ago. What was he working on, Harris?'

The Exploration Manager shook his head, but his eyes were wild. 'I've no idea what you're talking about!'

Crow waited for a few moments, his deep-set eyes boring into Harris's, his mouth set grimly. Then, in a soft voice, he said, 'Before I ask you once more, I'll remind you of a few things. This is a murder investigation; the body was found on site; the murderer is probably someone who knows the site; the motive is as yet unknown and you have, in my view, deliberately falsified a report from the dead man. That could mean you have also suppressed something. Since the man died only weeks later, I'm prepared to make the supposition that there's a connection between his death, the suppression of information regarding his work in early February, and the falsification of this report.' Crow tapped it with a bony finger. 'So, young man, I'll ask you again, now that you know the direction in which my mind is moving, *what was he working on?*'

Harris stood up violently, his chair crashing backwards.

His face was heavy with anger, his mouth working with emotions too big for him to control. He rubbed at his wrinkled forehead with a vague desperation as though he could thereby eradicate his problems, and he strode across to the window, glaring out at the lashing rain. He stood there for several minutes, as though thrashing over difficulties he could not surmount, and then he swung around to face Crow. His voice was bitter.

'This job . . . this project . . . it could make me, do you understand that? To reach Exploration Manager at my age in the Streisman Corporation — I could pick up an operations job anywhere in the world after this was successfully completed! And I believe in its viability! The publicity we've put out — the work we've put in to overcome environmental problems — we believed in it, Fred and I, we were equally committed to it. We both wanted it to succeed!'

He paused, shedding his anger suddenly, the violence and passion draining away from him as he walked back, leaden-footed to his desk. 'Then Fred came to me, last December. He was worried; he talked it over with me. That notebook, the one you found at his cottage. He showed it to me. The data—'

'The drilling data, and that relating to the ore concentration?'

'That's right. We . . . we said they were wrong. They aren't. They're damn right.'

'Are you telling me the senior management lied to me over that data when I asked—'

Harris shook his head. 'No. They were proceeding on the assumption that figures already supplied to them were accurate. Only . . . only I knew they were wrong.'

Crow's tone was cool. 'You said nothing at the time. Indeed, you—'

'I know. I insisted they were accurate. But by then I had to. Because I'd seen the rest of Fred's report, the work, the foraging he'd done in early February . . .'

Crow sighed. 'He showed you a report . . . gave it to you . . . and you suppressed it?'

Harris nodded. His face was grey. 'I'd asked him to give me time to consider it. I held it for a couple of weeks; we had a session over it and we . . . disagreed about its use. He wanted to mail it to Myron Streisman, and wanted my support. I played for time while I tried to persuade him there was another way to handle things. Then . . . then he was killed. And I was left with the report. So . . . so I did nothing about it. And in case questions were asked I filed an older report, as you guessed, with a new date, and put it in to Grainger, so it would be a double check.'

'You still have the report Norman made in February?' Crow asked.

Harris nodded miserably. 'I have it at home.'

'All right, Harris, so what was so important about the Norman report that you needed to suppress it?'

Harris glared at Crow as though he thought the policeman could not have been listening to him. 'But don't you understand? Fred had gone over the top in that report! He knew the project was viable! He knew its importance for the county, and for the country as well! And damn it all, he knew how important it was for me, too! Yet he was insisting that it went in to Streisman — and that would have blown the whole project wide open! At the very least it would have led to dismissals — at worst, it would have brought the whole project to an end. And he was prepared to do this, just for the sake of . . . hell, I don't know . . . conscience . . . justice . . . a refusal to accept the realities of business life . . . It could have been dealt with quietly, I could have seen Grainger, but no, Fred wanted to explode the whole thing. Righteous bloody indignation, that's what it was, and it would have cost me my job and my prospects! That's why I suppressed it! And I'd do the same again!'

Crow was silent for a little while, staring at the wild-eyed man facing him. 'You suppressed the report after he was killed, you said.'

'That's right.'

'And the copy you have — it was the only extant copy?'

'Of course it . . . well, yes, I . . . I'm pretty sure it was.'

'And if it wasn't . . . ?' Crow watched the man carefully for several seconds. 'For it occurs to me, Mr Harris, that if there was another copy, and if it *was* as important as you make out . . .'

Pete Harris knew exactly what he was saying: if the report was that important, someone might have killed to suppress it. And his eyes told John Crow that Harris had also followed the underlying suspicion — if there was only one copy, could the Exploration Manager have killed to keep the report under cover?

* * *

Delaval was late arriving at the hotel for dinner, and Crow had no idea when to expect him, so he had dinner alone. While he ate, with an indifferent hock to wash down a doubtful Dover sole, he read once more the report that Fred Norman had been working on before he died. The hotel restaurant was quiet — though Crow had gathered from the reception desk that the hotel would be fully booked during the royal visit — and he had a table in the corner, near the window, where he could remain undisturbed, and he went through the report very carefully. In a sense it raised for him more problems than it provided answers, though it certainly explained why Pete Harris wanted to suppress it. His motives were clear-cut; nevertheless, the question remained whether he had merely suppressed it after Norman's death — or had done something more positive before that time.

The waiter who approached his table was slim and obsequious. Crow thought for a moment he was simply coming to ask whether the meal had been to Crow's liking; instead, it was to inform him that he was wanted on the telephone. With a grunt, Crow lurched to his feet: he disliked having a meal interrupted in this manner, and he could guess who it was. He followed the waiter, who pointed to the kiosk in the hallway. Crow entered it, closed the door behind him, and, when the switchboard buzzed, picked up the phone.

'Delaval? Where the hell are you?'

'I beg your pardon?' The voice at the other end of the crackling line was unfamiliar. 'Is that Detective Superintendent Crow?'

'Oh, I beg *your* pardon; I thought it was a colleague. Yes, my name is Crow.'

'And my name is Jenkins. Did you receive safely the report I sent down from Bristol? On the data produced for the Streisman Corporation?'

Crow frowned, at a loss for a moment. He cleared his throat. 'Mr Jenkins . . . do you work at the Bristol forensic laboratories?'

'Yes, I'm sorry, I should have explained.' The line crackled violently, so Crow lost the next few words. ' . . . prepared it, and I thought I'd check to see if it was what you wanted.'

'Yes, thank you,' Crow replied. 'It was fine. You . . . er . . . you answered a problem for me, or rather, supported a suspicion I held.'

'I'm pleased.' There was a short, awkward pause. 'I . . . I'm staying overnight in Exeter, — I'm due to give evidence for the police in a drunken driving case tomorrow — paint scrapings and all that sort of thing, though why they weren't satisfied with the usual affidavit I don't know and I wondered if we might be able to have a brief talk.'

Crow hesitated. 'I don't know that it will be necessary, Mr Jenkins. Your report was admirable, and—'

'No, I don't make myself clear. I'd like to have a chat with you . . . it's on something that isn't connected with the report I sent you, but it's been worrying me and . . .' His voice tailed away, as though he were suddenly embarrassed.

'Tomorrow's a bit difficult—'

'I'm here for three days, I would think,' Jenkins said eagerly. 'How about Friday?'

Crow hesitated, and thought quickly. 'Friday . . . I'm afraid I have an important appointment at ten a.m., but maybe if we could meet before then? I shall certainly be in Exeter that day.'

'Perhaps over an early cup of coffee, Superintendent? Just opposite the Guildhall, a coffee-house in the Cathedral Close. Say half past nine. It shouldn't take us long.'

'All right. But I'll have to leave by about nine-fifty, to get to Glassland headquarters.'

'As I said, Superintendent Crow, it shouldn't take us long . . .'

Crow replaced the phone, frowning in puzzlement. He could not imagine what more Jenkins might want to tell him about the report . . . but had he not said it had nothing to do with the report he'd sent from Bristol? In Crow's experience forensic scientists were a strange bunch: they tended to be prickly in their relationships with police officers, at least if they considered their professional judgments were in danger of being twisted or directed, and they did not offer theories readily — only facts. Admirable, in a sense, but sometimes frustrating, though Crow himself had always respected their independence of mind and action. He walked back to the dining-room and saw that his table was now occupied by Inspector Delaval.

'Hello, sir. I gathered you'd finished but for coffee, so I took the liberty of ordering you a brandy. Saw you on the phone. Wife?'

Crow shook his head. 'No. Chap from the Bristol labs. Where the hell have you been?'

'Working hard, sir.' Delaval looked as though he had: there were tired lines around his eyes, and some of his normal freshness seemed to have disappeared. 'Just finished a while ago. Had a sandwich, so no appetite now. But a drink, that's another thing. Ah . . .'

The waiter was approaching with two double brandies.

Delaval took his and sipped it, nodding, then added some ginger ale to it, to Crow's disapproval. He looked up and grinned shamefacedly. 'I know, sir, but upper-class habits come hard to a boy from Byker. How did you get on today, out at Ottershaw?'

Crow smiled. 'Well enough . . . and interestingly enough. But I have a suspicion that you have something to tell me — so my news can wait. You managed to open up some other lines of enquiry at Exeter?'

'I think so.'

'Brigadier Leveson?'

'The very same.' Delaval leaned back in his chair, relaxing, as the waiter approached with Crow's coffee. 'You might remember,' he continued, 'that I felt uneasy about my talk with Brigadier Leveson. To begin with, I wasn't convinced that he was really bothered about environmental considerations on his estate: his argument that he was against Streisman's reopening of the shaft on his land because it would destroy the character of the estate seemed a bit hollow to me. Particularly since he didn't seem to give a damn about the Ottershaw traffic problem. Secondly, he wouldn't contemplate severance of the options Streisman has over his land and thirdly, well, I got the impression he wasn't unhappy that negotiations with Fred Norman broke down.'

'If I may interrupt you there,' Crow said, 'I've learned that the breakdown arose not because Myron Streisman vetoed the royalty deal, but because the shape of the ore body meant the tongue of land owned by Leveson wouldn't be needed.'

Delaval pursed his mouth thoughtfully, and his blue eyes were cold. 'That wasn't the impression Leveson left with me.

What I *did* feel was that for some reason he was trying to damage the whole enterprise with the court action and the planning enquiry or at the least, slow it down. And there was also the issue of Norman's diary—'

'You mean the fact that Norman noted a visit to Leveson in February?'

Delaval nodded. 'Right. The Brigadier told me he had *summoned* Norman on January 25 and negotiations broke down. Why did Norman go back? Leveson never mentioned a later meeting. Maybe it was because Norman went back with more cards in his hand, cards Brigadier Leveson didn't want exposed.'

'And your work in Exeter—'

'Proved productive, sir. I managed to discover what Norman had been up to. He spent some time at the Streisman headquarters, using their research staff — he made contact with the Companies Registry; and he spent some time in the public library in the city. So I followed him around, retraced his steps, and, eventually, discovered the cards he had unearthed.' He wrinkled his nose. 'You remember the conversation we had with Ray Grainger, first visit we had to the site?'

'When he showed us around the plant?'

'That's right. Well, he told it to us that day, in a nutshell, though inadvertently. It all goes back to the old days and a story of lost opportunities. Technical innovations in the use of tungsten in alloys made by the Germans raised the price of the commodity before the First World War, and the war itself pushed prices higher, so the old workings were started. In the mid-thirties the Carter Syndicate was formed — mainly local businessmen and a few landowners — but never did very much until it was too late. In 1967 Mr Myron Streisman showed up. It was a gamble on his part — but he was prepared to wait for the right time to come along. He bought up the Carter lease, but didn't begin the exploration programme until recently.'

'So where does that leave us?' Crow asked.

'One of Brigadier Leveson's particular gripes is that his uncle, who owned the estates before him, had been conned by Streisman. I couldn't see it that way: it seemed to me to be a matter of straightforward dealing—'

'In the best Streisman tradition,' Crow added, smiling.

'—and paying £200,000 for rights of way seemed to be pretty reasonable to me, too. So the word conned was harsh, I felt. Unless you see the whole thing in its true perspective.'

'And you now have the perspective?'

'I think so. It wasn't that Leveson's uncle was conned at all. It's merely that Brigadier Leveson is sore about the missed opportunity bit.'

'I don't understand.'

Delaval finished his brandy with a flourish. 'The Brigadier's uncle — and the family before him — had major shareholdings in the Carter Syndicate. When they sold the lease to Streisman they were throwing away what'll prove to be a gold-mine—'

'*Wolframite* mine.'

'You know what I mean: I was speaking figuratively,' Delaval said, and grinned. '*That's* what Leveson is sore about, and why he's bitter about Streisman and his corporation. He feels the Syndicate should have been operating the site, not this American company. Once I reached that conclusion, it was just a matter of talking to the Public Trustee, and getting some other interesting information.'

'Which was?'

'That the Carter Syndicate shares were liquidated and placed in a trust fund, which can't be touched for another thirty years, unless they are used for a particular eventuality.'

'Tell me.'

'The reopening of the mining operations at Ottershaw.'

Crow frowned, puzzled. 'But that's not possible now — the Streisman Corporation has the lease.'

'Ah. That's where things become really interesting,' Delaval said. 'Streisman took the remainder of the existing lease in 1968. It amounted to a run of fourteen years.'

'And at the end of that period?'

'There are two possibilities. Streisman can renew the lease entirely — and there is a clause that states he has this option if he has made the mining viable — or it can revert to the Carter Syndicate, who would be able through their trustees to renegotiate with Streisman, or start mining for themselves again.'

'But if Streisman had made the whole thing almost viable by then, it would seen inequitable that the Carter group could just come in and take over,' Crow demurred.

'I agree. I think it would give rise to a legal battle, which Streisman could well win. But what if he hadn't proved it viable, because he hadn't had time to do so?'

'You mean,' Crow said slowly, 'if the venture had been delayed, slowed down by court action and planning enquiries to such an extent that no commercial mining had taken place before the lease was renewable?'

'Exactly. Things would have taken a different slant then. The Carter trustees could point to a fourteen-year lease under which Myron Streisman had given off a lot of hot air about what he would do for the British economy, but had produced very little — so why not give a British company a chance to do what he hadn't?'

'The trustees of the Carter group shares—'

'It's in the hands of the Public Trustee,' Delaval interrupted. 'Who'll act in the best interests of his beneficiaries.'

'And I can guess who one of those beneficiaries will be.'

'More to the point, perhaps,' Delaval said, 'Fred Norman guessed. He did all the spadework on this one: he was angry, and he was suspicious because of the breakdown of negotiations with the Brigadier. So he hunted around. And he found all this out, and he learned who the major beneficiary of the trust fund was — a trust fund that couldn't be touched for thirty years except under a renewal of the mining at Ottershaw.'

'And that's why he went to see Brigadier Leveson on February 17?'

Delaval nodded. 'That'll be my guess. He went to tell him he knew all about the Carter Syndicate situation; that he knew Leveson was a major beneficiary under the trust; that if Leveson didn't withdraw his court action against the options, pull out his objections in the planning enquiry, agree the options and the road construction, he'd publicly declare the Brigadier's interest — and that would be enough to scotch the court action to start with, and maybe the planning enquiry too. In other words, pull back quietly, or have a public slanging match which would also count against Leveson when the lease came up for renewal.'

'I get the feeling, more and more, that Mr Norman could be so committed to matters of principle that he would be a difficult man to live with,' Crow said quietly.

'Brigadier Leveson may well have thought so,' Delaval replied. His icy blue eyes met Crow's. 'But then, Leveson doesn't have to live with Fred Norman any more, does he?'

Crow sat silent for a little while, thinking. He sipped his coffee; across the table, Delaval waited, without speaking. At last, Crow sighed. 'All right. I'll fill you in now on this report—' he tapped it with his bony finger — 'and what I learned today from our friend Pete Harris. But before I do, are you really of the opinion that we need to ask more questions of Brigadier Leveson?' He hesitated. 'I mean, do you really think he had sufficient motivation for killing Fred Norman?'

'All I know,' Delaval said stubbornly, 'is that the Streisman Corporation will be sinking perhaps eight million pounds into Ottershaw. They expect to make a handsome profit at the end of the day, supported by Government subsidy. That kind of profit could be siphoned towards the Carter Syndicate beneficiaries — as well as releasing money that's otherwise tied up for thirty years. If that isn't a sound enough motive for removing someone who could scotch all your plans—'

Crow raised a hand in an admission of defeat. 'I think your point is made. And now it's your turn to listen . . .'

CHAPTER 5

The early morning sky was a pale, washed-out blue, veined with a fine tracery of clouds, and along the riverside the hum of the city traffic was muted. The Exe was high, swollen from the rains two days earlier, but bright sunshine warmed John Crow's back as he paced along the bank towards the canal. He had slept badly and risen early; leaving Delaval at the hotel, he had been out at seven-thirty, to walk through a quiet Cathedral Close, down the narrowness of Stepcote Hill, and listen to the echo of his footsteps along the deserted nineteenth century quayside flanked by warehouses. He strolled along towards the lock-house and toll house at Turf, but was hardly aware of his surroundings: his mind was still on the investigation he was conducting. He was bothered by a vague feeling of dissatisfaction; an anxiety that he was reaching dead ends in the work he and Delaval were carrying out. It might have been conditioned by the experiences of yesterday: they had driven out to Brigadier Leveson's estate only to learn that the ex-Army officer had gone to London, and the menservants they questioned were unable to give an address. Delaval had suggested, impetuously, that they should put out a police call for the apprehension of the Brigadier, but that was too premature. It might, on the other hand, be due to the reluctance he felt to meet Myron Streisman and Edward Foster, MP, at the Streisman headquarters that morning. For, in a curious way, he was nearer to solving the American businessman's problems than his own — which might please Myron Streisman, but certainly did not make the morning happier for John Crow.

He glanced at his watch. He had told Delaval of his appointment in the Cathedral Close at nine-thirty, and had suggested Delaval come along. It was time he now retraced his steps to return up Fore Street to keep his appointment. He made his way back along the riverside, turned up past the stepped sidewalks and central cobbled gutters of the steeply rising road at Stepcote until he was able to turn into Fore Street. He caught sight of the Guildhall some five minutes before he was due for his appointment, and in the Cathedral Close, outside the cafe, Delaval was already waiting.

'No breakfast this morning, sir?'

'Orange juice was enough. And then a walk. But a coffee would go down well, now.'

The staff were not too pleased, it seemed, that they were expected to serve upstairs so soon in the morning, but there was only a short wait before they brought two coffees to the two men as they sat in a dark oak window-seat overlooking the close, and awaited the man from Bristol.

He arrived punctually, just three minutes after the coffee, extending a soft, pudgy hand, introducing himself as Arnold Jenkins, and giving Crow the impression of a nervous soft-bodied hen, red-faced, tiny button eyes, the sprays of hair sprouting from his ears subsidizing the thinning areas on his head. He sat down, and Crow ordered a coffee for him before introducing Delaval. Then they waited, but the nervous little forensic scientist seemed in no hurry to begin.

'I like cathedrals,' he said, nodding in the direction of the building across the green close. 'That's a fine one except for the blunder in the west front. You seen it? They tried to create a great screen for sculpture, in the manner of Salisbury, but the panelled walls, they just emphasize the falsity of the device. Yes, an artistic blunder . . .'

His voice died away as the two policemen remained silent. Crow glanced at his watch. 'I'm sorry, Mr Jenkins, it would be nice to talk to an enthusiast about his interest in cathedrals, but we have only ten or fifteen minutes before we're due at another appointment—'

'Quite so, quite so,' Jenkins said urgently. 'I appreciate the situation. My interest in churches . . . and a certain reluctance, I suppose, to raise other matters . . .'

Crow glanced at Delaval. 'Reluctance? What do you mean? Have you found out anything else about that Streisman report I sent you?'

'Well, no,' Jenkins admitted unhappily. 'But it wasn't the report I wanted to talk to you about. And my reluctance . . . well, you know how it is with us people, Superintendent. We have a difficult job to do, and it isn't helped by police officers who try to tell us what we should find, instead of letting us tell them what we *have* found. A good liaison officer helps, but very often someone will come in and pull rank, and there's trouble . . .' He paused, his little button eyes searching earnestly the faces of the two men with him, looking for signs of sympathy. 'It gets worse,' he went on, 'when some of your findings are ignored.'

Crow hesitated, then leaned forward to stir his coffee. 'I know what you mean,' he said, 'but you should also see the other side of things. Some information you give the police can't be used for a number of reasons . . . or it's deemed politic to make no reference to it—'

'But isn't that suppression of evidence?' Jenkins asked with a note of excitement in his voice. 'Wouldn't you agree it's suppression of evidence?'

Crow was taken aback. 'I'm not prepared to generalize about things like that, Mr Jenkins. You'd have to be more specific. And even then, unless one knows the full facts of a case, it's difficult to express an opinion—'

'You're involved with events at the Streisman site, up at Ottershaw.'

'We're investigating the murder of Fred Norman, yes. Have you any particular information regarding that?'

'No, no.' Jenkins shook his head violently. 'I did some work on that case, but it's not that I wanted to talk about. It's the way the police handled that other incident up at Ottershaw.'

'What other incident?' Crow asked.

'The death of that girl in the street accident.'

Crow stared at the forensic scientist, and the man's little eyes wavered before his own. 'You mean Freda Park?' Crow asked.

'That's right.' As Delaval shifted uncomfortably in the window-seat, Jenkins squirmed also in a sudden embarrassment. 'You see, I don't consider the police used my report properly. I . . . I consider they did not take note of it in its entirety.'

Crow stared at his coffee cup. He realized now why the little man was embarrassed. He wasn't quite certain what Jenkins was suggesting, but he *was* talking to an outsider, not a member of the investigating force, and that could have repercussions. He shook his head regretfully. 'I'm not sure that you should be talking to me, you know we're not involved in that hit-and-run investigation and—'

'But you *are* working up at Ottershaw,' Jenkins insisted, 'and I feel that if you knew the full facts, at the appropriate time you might speak to the officers concerned.'

Crow finished his coffee. 'No, I don't think that's a very sensible—'

'Perhaps we ought to hear what Mr Jenkins has to say, sir,' Delaval suggested, and Crow turned to him in surprise. The northerner met his glance briefly, but Crow read nothing from the glance; he suspected Delaval was motivated merely by curiosity, but he could not now bring himself to tell the young inspector, curtly, that he should follow the lead given by the senior officer. But in private, later . . . Crow nodded to Arnold Jenkins. 'All right. Tell us what the problem is.'

Now that he had the opportunity, Jenkins seemed to be wavering. He hesitated, his button eyes glancing out towards the sunshine of the close and the cathedral beyond. Then he sighed. 'Well, I suppose it's nothing, really, but I did the post-mortem on the Park girl and I made a full report. Some of it was used, but other parts of it were not acted upon, and when I was back home — I'm from Elburton, just outside Plymouth, you see — from what I could hear, not even rumour had raised the matter, so I guess the police had . . . suppressed it.'

'Suppressed what?' Crow asked quietly.

'The fact that Freda Park was not a virgin.'

Arnold Jenkins stared earnestly at John Crow as though hoping he would express shock and dismay; instead, Crow took a deep breath. 'I . . . I think that *suppression* is rather a harsh word to use regarding evidence which is . . . shall we say . . . of little or even no relevance to an enquiry.'

Arnold Jenkins expressed bewilderment. 'But I can't agree! I mean, I know maybe it *is* of no relevance, but there appears to have been no . . .' He shook his head, as though trying to clear it. 'I've obviously not explained myself properly. Let me start again . . . I did the post-mortem. Freda Park was killed by a hit-and-run driver: the pelvis was crushed, the upper chest smashed, fragments of bone entered the lungs and heart, and the skull suffered multiple fractures. She would have been dead before the ambulance arrived; the vehicle which hit her would have been travelling at some speed, and I gather there was no attempt made to slow or stop.'

'What's her virginity got to do with that?' Delaval asked.

'Well, nothing, I suppose,' Jenkins said helplessly. 'But a scientist looks at *all* the facts and I'm just disturbed that . . . you see, gentlemen, the crushing of the pelvis and the lower body caused problems, but it doesn't destroy the validity of my findings, namely, that some short interval before her death, Freda Park had had sexual intercourse. There were traces of semen—'

'I'm sorry, Mr Jenkins,' Crow began, rising to his feet and glancing again at his watch, but we do have an appointment and—'

'No, please, let me finish,' Jenkins insisted. 'That wasn't all, you see; that wasn't the summation of my findings. The hypothesis—'

'Tell us, Mr Jenkins,' Delaval said.

'I don't believe the act took place with her consent,' Jenkins declared defiantly.

Crow sat down. He looked at Delaval, and something moved deep inside those pale blue eyes, a shimmering of excitement. He turned back to Jenkins. 'Explain yourself.'

Arnold Jenkins took a deep breath. 'I admit there is a problem. The lower body was crushed; the pelvis, the thighs . . . but it is my opinion . . . my *professional* opinion . . . that shortly before her death Freda Park was party to certain violent sexual activity.'

'That isn't exactly what you said a moment ago,' Crow said. 'You suggested she was *forced*—'

Jenkins waved unhappy hands. 'You must understand . . . the damage done by the accident . . . it caused problems. But I felt in my examination that the bruising of the thighs, the tears of the vaginal wall, the presence of semen and the scratch marks—'

'Scratches?' Delaval repeated in surprise.

'That's one of the points I stress,' Jenkins explained. 'Scratching of that kind is *possible* in an accident, but I have dealt with questions of sexual assault and rape in the past and the degree of skin damage is consistent with—'

'Let's get this straight,' Crow interrupted impatiently. 'Are you saying that Freda Park was *raped* before she was killed in that accident?'

The hands fluttered again, in vague desperation. 'No, I'm not saying that, Superintendent Crow. The results of the post-mortem are . . . inconclusive in that respect. The accident

. . . But the point is, I did include in my report statements concerning these sexual injuries, but they don't seem to have been followed up in any way. All the information I have received since would suggest that the police have treated this as a straightforward hit-and-run case—'

'And you're saying it wasn't?'

'No!' Arnold Jenkins was beginning to become angry at what he saw as obtuseness on Crow's part. 'Don't you understand? I'm not saying *anything!* I'm making no statements regarding a hypothesis — I'm simply giving you facts — facts which, it seems to me, the local police investigation ignored. And that's why I come to you. With your experience . . . with your knowledge . . .'

'Mr Jenkins,' Crow said softly, 'I don't wish to cavil, but you can hardly expect the police to follow up evidence you produce if you put it in such a negative way.'

'The evidence is there,' Jenkins reiterated stubbornly. 'It's for the police to draw conclusions, put them to me, and I will then support or reject them — on the basis of the evidence and my expertise. But the questions have never been asked. That concerns me. And I want to know why they've not been asked!'

Crow stood up again, towering over the little man. He considered what to say for a few moments, then gently he said, 'There are a number of reasons why it might not have been followed up, Mr Jenkins. In the first instance, the local police investigating the incident might have considered the evidence too flimsy to proceed on — you say yourself there are problems because of the extent of the injuries caused by the hit-and-run accident. Secondly, they may have felt the situation was irrelevant — they are looking for a hit-and-run merchant, not looking into the sexual predilections of a young girl — which could have been violent by her own demands. And you must also remember her age — she was fifteen. It may be that the police took into account the feelings of her mother.'

Arnold Jenkins wrinkled his brow. 'I don't understand.'

'Mrs Park had lost her daughter in an accident. She was just fifteen. It *may* be the local police felt that she was suffering enough distress — they wouldn't want to add to it by raising other issues that they might not in any case be able to prove. They'd gain nothing — and Mrs Park could well suffer a great deal more distress unnecessarily.'

Jenkins jutted a stubborn lower lip. 'I accept what you say, but I am a scientist and my duty—'

'I'm sorry,' Crow said brusquely, beginning to lose patience. I have another appointment. Delaval—'

The detective inspector looked up and nodded. 'I'll join you in a few minutes, sir. I think it would be best if I heard Mr Jenkins out, got details of the evidence he points to, and then maybe we'll be able to make enquiries later.'

Crow nodded. That was the sensible course. It would mollify the forensic scientist at little cost to themselves and if anything *did* come of it they could pass a hint to the local police, once their own investigation into the Norman murder was completed. If it was *ever* completed, he thought bitterly. The way things were going . . . He nodded to Delaval again. 'Fine. I'll see you shortly, then.'

He said goodbye to Arnold Jenkins and went downstairs to pay for the coffee at the desk. As he left, in the quiet of the early-morning coffee-house he could hear Arnold Jenkins's urgent though muffled tones beating at Delaval's reluctant ears.

* * *

Crow arrived two or three minutes late at the headquarters of the Streisman Corporation, but it made no difference, for he was kept waiting in an ante-room for some twenty minutes before a pert secretary finally ushered him through the panelled doors into the executive suite of the company, reserved, it would seem, for those occasions on which Myron Streisman visited Exeter. The room was carpeted in thick pile, modern paintings adorned the walls, the furniture was massive and expensive, and the view over the city and the moors at Haldon was fine. Edward Foster was already seated in a deep chair near the window, and he made no attempt to rise to greet Crow as he came in; Myron Streisman was already on his feet, prowling as ever, and looking sternly towards the tall skeletal figure of the man approaching him. His bright narrow eyes glittered. 'Superintendent Crow. How have things been going?'

There were to be no preliminaries. Crow raised an eyebrow, quizzically. 'Going? At the pilot plant, or in the investigation I'm conducting?'

'They're one and the same thing,' Streisman rasped. 'I asked you—'

'I clearly recall what you asked me to do, Mr Streisman,' Crow interrupted. 'I made no promise to undertake the task of . . . investigating your company, beyond what I found necessary to do in discovering the murderer of Fred Norman.'

'You've found him?' Foster queried sharply, his handsome head coming up as he stared at Crow.

Crow smiled thinly. 'Far from finding the identity of Norman's killer, I don't even know *why* Norman was killed.'

'Well, you don't seem to have been getting much done down here,' Foster expostulated, 'in spite of the assurances given us by Commander Gray. He as good as said—'

'Will you clear this matter up before the opening of the pilot plant?' Streisman interrupted impatiently.

'I don't think there's the remotest chance of that happening,' Crow admitted.

Foster snorted in annoyance. 'So you've damn all to report!'

'The superintendent didn't say that,' Streisman objected. He was staring at John Crow, aware of the hostility in Crow's bearing, and suspecting that the policeman's controlled anger was really directed inwards. 'I have the feeling he *does* have something to report to us.'

Crow nodded. 'You might not be happy with what you hear.'

'Business isn't about happiness,' Streisman replied shortly.

Crow inclined his head. 'All right. The fact of the matter is, you requested that I investigate your company as well as this murder. I had no intention of doing that but, in making enquiries into Norman's death, certain facts have come to light which . . . to say the least . . . may well be of interest to you.'

'So fire away.'

'May I sit down?' Streisman looked surprised at the request, but nodded, and when Crow settled down in an armchair the American businessman moved around the room, pacing on his short legs, quick, restless steps that drew the eyes of both his companions. Crow leaned forward. 'I think you told me yourself that there was too much trouble with the operation at Ottershaw.'

'A feeling I had. A sense. You can confirm it?'

'It seems to me, as an outsider, that there are several major problems affecting the firm,' Crow replied. 'In the first instance, in spite of the very hard and committed work undertaken by Fred Norman, there is a build-up of considerable opposition on environmental grounds to the project.'

'This Action Group from the village?' Streisman shook his head. 'We can handle screwballs like that.'

'Don't underestimate them. They might yet cause you trouble — but apart from that, you're not simply going to dismiss the opposition of Brigadier Leveson. But I can advise you that there is a way to handle it.'

Streisman's little eyes shot a keen glance in Crow's direction. 'Leveson? How?'

'We can't take the credit for it. It was something Norman had discovered before he died — he just hadn't had time to inform you. It's simply this: Leveson has a financial interest in stopping the project, or at the very least slowing it down. If he can do either, he'll probably try to revive the fortunes of the Carter Syndicate by establishing a similar project under a new lease — or else make you pay through the nose for a new lease.'

Streisman nodded thoughtfully. 'The leasing arrangements . . . I'd wondered. All right, go on.'

Crow leaned back in his chair, relaxing. In a strange way he was beginning to enjoy himself: it was rather satisfying to be able to sit here telling a big businessman like Myron Streisman just what was wrong with his company — and the men he had picked to run it for him. If only Martha could see him now, in this unaccustomed role . . .'I think you've made a mistake in the way you've set up the Ottershaw operation.'

Edward Foster was staring at Crow as though he could hardly believe his ears. Streisman himself stopped pacing. He stared at Crow, calculations dancing in his eyes. 'What's that supposed to mean?'

'As I understand the workings of business, they're no different from any other organization — the police, for instance — in certain respects. The principles of delegation must be applied to achieve the best results.'

'That's so, but—'

'Basic to any such system, however, is that the delegation not only occurs, but is exercised in regard to the appropriate people. Equally basic is the fact that the exercise of the delegated functions is monitored in an effective way.'

Streisman ran pudgy hands down over the front of his dark grey suit. He frowned. 'You're implying that this hasn't been done in my organization?'

'I am. To start with, you've operated a particular system of appointments which is . . . idiosyncratic to say the least.' He heard a slight hiss of indrawn breath from Edward Foster, but drove on. 'You've appointed as managers men who are loners to a large extent, who have no secure marital backgrounds, and this, *you* seem to believe, makes them better managers, because they commit themselves wholly to the company.'

'You don't agree?' Streisman asked.

'It *can* work,' Crow admitted. 'Maybe it worked with Fred Norman — he certainly drove himself hard for you.

But it can also raise tensions, increase the loneliness and frustrations of the men concerned, and perhaps make their tensions turn inwards, multiply and, ultimately, lead to inefficiency in running the business.'

'I presume,' Streisman said harshly, 'you have facts to support these . . . ah . . . theories?'

Crow shrugged. 'It's obvious your managers don't work as a team. They tend to work in isolated boxes, each to his own task. It meant, for instance, that no one really knew what Norman was working on during the weeks before his death. It meant that reports were not normally routed to Ray Grainger, even though he is Project Manager — only specific reports were sent to him — and then, it seems, he doesn't read them.'

'You mean that Grainger has delegated too much to the others?' Streisman demanded.

'It's a view,' Crow suggested, 'and one I would not dissent from. I'm only an outsider—'

'But objective,' Streisman interrupted. 'Go on.'

'All right. There is a more serious aspect to the whole thing, however, and one which underlines not only what I mean, but the extent of near-paranoia your system can inculcate. I've now found out just what Norman *was* working on shortly before his death. He was producing a report on the activities undertaken by your sub-contractor, Craydon Engineering.'

Streisman frowned. 'That kind of monitoring wouldn't have been in his brief.'

'But no one else was doing it,' Crow explained. 'And Norman obviously felt — as a corporation man — strongly about it. He must have come across drilling discrepancies as he went about his own environmental monitoring; he found errors in some reports on mineral concentrations. He noted them, dug a bit deeper, and came up with some disturbing ideas.'

'Such as?'

Crow crossed his legs at the ankles and stared down at his feet. 'In essence, that they were incompetent, or—'

'Or what?'

'Or that they were deliberately misleading.'

Edward Foster moved in his chair, sitting upright. Anger stained his eyes, but there was a nervous flicker in his tone as he spoke. 'Now look here. I can't accept that you should make statements like that—'

Myron Streisman raised a hand. 'Craydon Engineering were recommended to us by Mr Foster,' he said drily. 'They're a leading West Country firm—'

'But incompetent — or worse,' Streisman cut in acidly.

'That's the view reported by Fred Norman,' Crow said with care, noting that as the anger receded in Foster's eyes, so the hints of nervous tension grew. 'But he had other things to say, also.'

'Connected with Craydon Engineering?'

Crow nodded. 'He suggested in his report that they'd been cutting corners, financially, on some of their operations, but putting in larger bills of costs. They had highlighted certain drilling reports, claiming higher concentrates — and suggesting further drillings in new test areas. In other words, their reports demanded an extension of their work on site — and this was being acquiesced in by Ray Grainger.'

Myron Streisman was breathing heavily. 'Are you telling me Ray Grainger is finagling with the Craydon people?'

Crow folded his arms. 'That's not for me to say. Norman *hints* at it, but doesn't say so deliberately. He merely says an enquiry should be instituted.'

Foster stood up suddenly and walked forward. His voice trembled slightly. 'Myron, I had no idea that—' Streisman did not look at him. His eyes were cold and appraising as he continued to stare at Crow. 'Mr Foster,' he said, 'holds a consultancy post with Craydon Engineering. But we can *assume* that's neither here nor there. All right, Crow, this report — what happened to it?'

'It was suppressed.'

Myron Streisman balled his hand into a fist, but made no other move. 'By whom?' he asked distinctly, after a short silence.

'Your Exploration Manager, Pete Harris,' Crow said. 'His motives were clear enough, he says. Ottershaw was his big chance: he believes in the project. When Norman showed him the report — it was with Harris he worked more closely than anyone — and asked support in sending it to you, Harris prevaricated. He was afraid the report would end the project, that you'd come down like an avenging angel and sweep the whole thing clean, and this before the project — and Harris — had been proved. He held back on it — and then, when Norman was killed, he just suppressed it, hoping all would turn out well at the end, in spite of any finagling that Craydon had been up to.'

'I still can't believe it,' Foster muttered, his face white.

'I can,' Crow said patiently. 'The wrong kind of men working together. No reporting system. I even got two different stories — from Grainger, who should have known — and another source, concerning the withdrawal of mining from Leveson's tongue of land.'

'That was due to the shape of the ore body,' Streisman snapped.

'*Grainger* told me it was an instruction from you,' Crow explained. 'And he, if anyone, should have known! But that group — they just haven't been reporting to each other! And you can then understand Harris's actions more easily. He's obsessed with the successful completion of the project — and his own self-aggrandizement. He could see nothing wrong in suppressing the report, in condoning whatever kickbacks Craydon Engineering might be obtaining, in ignoring signs of Grainger's incompetence or worse — even in ignoring the implications of Norman's death! He was concerned only with looking inward — at his own position and the project itself.'

'I'll *have* him!' Streisman said in a cold voice that was the more menacing for its quietness. 'And after a full investigation I'll go through that project—'

Foster cleared his throat. 'If you don't mind my saying so, Myron, I think this had all better wait until after the opening of the pilot plant. I mean, so far, all we have is an account, second-hand from Superintendent Crow, of a report prepared by Fred Norman. We should not act precipitately. Television and radio coverage is already arranged for the ceremony; we have the meeting afterwards; we can expect some considerable newspaper publicity. If it gets out that you have, or are considering . . .'

Streisman glowered at him, his round face marked with distrust and anger. 'There'll be a *wide* accounting, Foster, believe me . . . but I agree, it must come *after* the ceremony.' He turned back to Crow. 'And you — *you* think my selection methods are bad.'

'Maybe you just struck unlucky with this bunch,' Crow said cheerfully.

'What you've said,' Streisman remarked thoughtfully, 'suggests to me that you've got a few ideas about Norman's murder, too.'

Crow's face was lugubrious as he stared back at Streisman, but he knew he was not fooling the man behind the Ottershaw project. Streisman was quick, perceptive, and intelligent. He would already have been weighing the odds, permutating the possibilities: Norman had found out about Leveson's self-interest before he died; it had also been before his death that the report had been shown to Harris — and both Harris and Grainger would have had good reason to want that report suppressed. Harris, Grainger, Leveson . . . Crow could see the questions in Streisman's piggy little eyes, but the questions were not asked. The head of the American corporation had weighed up the man facing him, and had respect for him: Crow had shown his firmness in London, and now he had shown this morning he cared nothing for the pressure that businessman or politician might be prepared to put on him.

He had his job to do, and he would do it according to his own lights. Myron Streisman respected that in a man.

* * *

'So we've two days until the official opening of the plant,' Crow said to Delaval. 'Monday morning, bright and shiny, they'll all be there.'

'How did Mr Streisman take what you had to say to him?' Delaval asked as he sat down opposite Crow in the Exeter office.

'A strange man — as he got angrier, he seemed to get colder,' Crow replied. 'I think heads will be rolling — after the ceremony, and if Norman's allegations are proved true. But there's another thing . . .'

'Yes, sir?'

Crow considered for a few moments. 'The revered Minister, Mr Edward Foster, MP — I got the impression he knew more about the business than one would have expected. It seems he was the party who recommended Craydon Engineering to Streisman, and he has a consultancy with them — and he was very quick to jump to their defence.' He paused again, thinking. 'I wonder what he'd have done if Craydon had got wind of Norman's report, and had told him about their fears? Or if Grainger had learned of it, and maybe approached Foster?' He smiled, suddenly. 'I'm getting fanciful again, young man. It comes of too close a proximity to you — I'm being corrupted.'

Delaval did not react; his cool blue eyes were shadowed. 'What did you make of that fellow Jenkins, sir?'

'Not much. Nor his story. I think—'

'I just wonder whether we might not ask around a bit about it.'

Crow looked at him, and shook his head. 'We've got enough on our plate already, without doing the job of the local police on a hit-and-run case.'

'But what if it wasn't a simple hit-and-run case?' Delaval persisted. 'The evidence that Jenkins unearthed—'

'Is inconclusive. Must be. The locals would have picked it up—'

'Unless they didn't for the reasons you mentioned, sir. But there's another perspective, isn't there?'

'And what might that be?'

Delaval shrugged and looked sheepishly at his superior officer. 'There's something I read once . . . it's to the effect that if you're placed at a great distance from an object, you're likely to be a bad judge of the relative space that separates other objects from it.'

Crow stared at Delaval; he had a glimmering of what Delaval was going to say, but he doubted the relevance of the comment to the enquiries they were making. He nodded. 'Go on.'

Encouraged, Delaval went on more quickly, 'It seems to me *we're* at a great distance from the object. We always are, I suppose, in any investigation. But normally, it doesn't matter too much. Here, I'm not so sure . . . There's Leveson, and there's Harris, and there's Grainger, each in their own little worlds, bound together, related, battling . . . but they are all tied together with one common cord.'

'The Ottershaw project?'

'That's right. The project draws them together, as it draws Jack Prince and Marlene Park together with Fred Norman. So we fix our attention on the narrowness of the space between them, in relation to the project—'

'Don't get too metaphysical with me, young man,' Crow warned.

'—and we assume there is an unspanned distance in other directions. We cannot see the bridge, the link, the *narrowness* of a distance — because we are too far away to judge the void that we assume separates them.'

'You've lost me,' Crow said flatly.

Delaval grinned shamefacedly. 'I'm a bit lost myself. But I have a feeling . . .'

'And you want to follow it up?'

Delaval nodded. 'A couple of days should do it. With some help—'

'I'll talk to Detective Inspector Carr. And you've got two days.'

* * *

They were two long days. With three men at his disposal, Delaval began again an exhaustive enquiry into the death of Freda Park. He followed up the report Jenkins had made and interviewed the officers on the case: he learned that it was the Chief Constable who had made the decision. The evidence was too inconclusive, the feelings of the mother were to be spared, the balance of probability was that it was a simple hit-and-run case.

He went through all the garage checks instituted by the police and drew a blank yet again. He sent two officers to check all paint and spray-gun sales at motor accessory shops in the area and he went once more over the statements made immediately after the accident.

It was all in vain. He had only a vague, unformed theory, but it simply did not hold water; he had no evidence to support it. And yet, if he tried to get closer, to cut down the distance, to get nearer the objects moving about in this community, tight, close-knit but with seeds of violence sprouting within . . .

On Sunday morning he paid another visit to Virginia Morgan. And on Monday, at midday he had found enough facts to fit his theory.

* * *

It was a bright morning, with high fleecy clouds shining against a sky so blue that Myron Streisman could have ordered it specially for the occasion of his triumph. A light breeze fluttered across the moorland, a warm touch to the skin, bringing a hint of spring, and the grass beyond the perimeter fence seemed alive with murmurings, soft and gentle, while larksong excited the air above the hill.

John Crow was at the site early. He had left Delaval at the office, vaguely excited about something, but yet unwilling to talk about it, waiting for phone calls to support whatever theories he had in mind. Crow himself had been busy enough during the last two days: Leveson had returned from London, and there had been an unpleasant interview in which the Brigadier had first denied the truth of the facts Crow put to him, then had blustered about privacy, and finally had admitted there to be a financial interest, to his benefit, in the Carter Syndicate. But when Crow had asked him if this had been the basis of his last conversation with Fred Norman he had fallen silent, his anger subsiding under the cooling hand of discretion. He had refused to answer any further questions without first consulting his solicitor; Crow, grim-faced, had promised him there *would* be further questions.

The session with Ray Grainger had been equally unpleasant, though in a rather different way. Crow had questioned him about his relationships with Craydon Engineering, and the sincerity had been wiped from Grainger's mouth as he had explained that his task was to monitor their activity and ensure publication of their findings. A general co-ordination, he had said, but his eyes were scared, and Crow had read panic in them when he asked Grainger if he had seen the Norman report on Craydon Engineering. Crow felt that the man could have been lying when he denied having seen it; he also felt that if Grainger had *not* seen it, at least he had a pretty good idea of what it might contain. Crow had left him disturbed and fretful: he heard him shouting at the self-effacing Janet as Crow left.

That left Pete Harris, but the Explorations Manager, a frown on his forehead and a slightly greenish pallor about his skin as though he had slept badly and drunk more than was good for him, was stubbornly sticking to the story he had already given John Crow. But perhaps even within the structured walls he had erected about himself, walls of self-deceit where he could argue that the only good was the completion of the project itself, he knew now that the blast of Myron Streisman's trumpet would soon bring crashing down all that was important to him: his dreams of his personal future.

Not one of them was concerned about what had happened to the man found dead in the tailings pond.

* * *

A car park had been set aside to the left of the entrance for the relatively unimportant; Crow had parked there, and was already getting his long legs disentangled prior to emerging when Alan Fairfield, the Transport Manager, greeted him.

'There's no need to park here, Superintendent. I thought you might be along, so I've reserved a space for you up with the bigwigs — across there, beside the ore-crushing plant. It's just a few steps from there to the reception area, where they've laid on the champers and salmon.' He looked around him, running a hand through his sandy, crinkly hair, and sniffing at the wind. 'Nice morning for it.'

Crow nodded, and started the car again. Fairfield pointed to where he suggested Crow park, and then added, 'I'll be across shortly, and show you where the reception's to be held. Another hour yet, though.'

Crow parked the car where he was directed and then took a short tour of the site, walking inside the perimeter fence, under the feed conveyor to the pilot plant, strolling among the ruined huts built by the Carter Syndicate years ago, and down along the primary crusher access road to the small rise in the ground where he could look out over the lifting moorland. The site behind him was quiet — work had been suspended, lorries banned in expectation of visitors' cars for the official opening, and if it had not been for the noise made by television crews setting up their equipment he could have forgotten, as he stared across the blue hills, the existence of the Ottershaw project.

And yet the tailings pond still lay there, and the man who had died there was still on John Crow's mind.

He turned, walked past the spoil-heap and the trench, past the hoist engine-house, and there was the mine water disposal area ahead of him, the tailings pond stagnant, murky, its edges scarred by the equipment that had been brought in to drag the pond after the discovery of Norman's body, but the whole area now settling again to a basic, functional appearance.

'Ugly place,' said the voice at his back.

Crow turned. It was Alan Fairfield, standing with his broad shoulders hunched, hands stuck in pockets. 'This is one place Ray Grainger *won't* let them photograph.'

'The television people and the newspapers want to shoot it?'

Fairfield nodded. 'Bloody ghouls. Not the kind of publicity Streisman's needs. And not the kind we're going to hand to them. I've made sure the parking system makes it damn difficult for them to get up here and—' He stopped speaking suddenly and cocked his head on one side, like an inquisitive terrier, thin-lipped, hard-eyed. He frowned, then shook his head before going on. 'Thought I could hear . . . Anyway, as I was saying, I've made sure the drilling rig has blocked off access by car to this area, except for that road beyond the hoist engine-house—'

Along which the corpse of Fred Norman had been driven.

'—and I've *persuaded* them to set up near the site marked out for the arrival of the White Chiefs.' He stared at Crow, a hint of hostility deep in his eyes. 'Why the hell Streisman and Foster couldn't come by car . . .'

'Makes better television,' Crow murmured.

'Mmmm.' Fairfield nodded, then hesitated before speaking again. 'I . . . I was down the Miner's Arms last night.'

'Yes?'

'They were all a bit quiet with me. Saying nothing, really — and I drink there pretty regular, know quite a few in the village. I got the feeling . . . You know there'll be hardly any local coppers out here today?'

'The Royal visit to Exeter.' Crow nodded. 'Just a token force.'

'Yeah, but that's the . . .' Fairfield broke off again, his narrow eyes squinting suddenly down the hill. 'You hear something? There's lorries . . . I told the bastards not to come near the place today. Those stupid . . .' He strode forward for a few yards, then broke into a half-run suddenly towards the engine-house. One hand on the stone wall, he looked down over the valley. A moment later he turned again and ran back towards John Crow. 'I knew it, damn them, I knew it! That bloody man Prince'll be behind this!'

'What's happening?' Crow called out as Fairfield ran past.

'Ottershaw — and those blasted Bristol Activists! They're coming up to take over the site!'

Moments later Crow himself heard them — not lorries, but cars. He remained where he was, watching the access road, and a few minutes later they came into sight, lurching and bumping over the track, churning through the muddy slope — Land-Rovers, cars, Range-Rovers, emblazoned with slogans and filled with demonstrators, doggedly ploughing up over the hill to the rear of the site.

Had they come up to the main gates, Fairfield could have blocked their entrance; here, where Fred Norman's killer had obtained access to the site, the demonstrators were able to enter easily. They could not *drive* on to the site itself, but they merely had to park along the access road and they would be able to walk towards the pilot plant. There would be little that Fairfield or anyone else could do to stop them.

The first of the vehicles drove up behind the hoist engine-house and parked; Crow watched while a group of young people debouched, then, when the car drew up behind them and its occupants emerged Crow turned and walked back towards the pilot plant. It would be fifteen or twenty minutes before the demonstrators could be sensibly grouped — unless they were extremely well organized — so there was time to see what the plant management had in mind to control the situation.

He found Fairfield in the office with Ray Grainger and Pete Harris. Grainger's face was grey, but his eyes were angry:

he was under pressure now, the result of the exposure of Norman's report, but the demonstration gave him something else to think about. Perhaps he felt that if he could handle this, Myron Streisman might yet be turned aside from a path of vengeance. The animated discussion broke off as Crow entered.

'Superintendent — is there any chance of getting more police reinforcements?' Grainger asked urgently.

'How many men are on site?'

'Just twelve,' Fairfield said in a grim tone. 'They're really here only as an escort for Foster, and they're going to be useless to stop a mob pouring in from the access road.'

'You're going to have a problem,' Crow agreed. 'There's a count of at least fifteen or twenty cars and Land-Rovers — so you can say, at a conservative estimate, there'll be maybe eighty demonstrators.'

Fairfield swore luridly and Grainger looked sick. Harris sat down; he seemed puzzled, as though all this could not really be happening, not to the site on which he had expended such energy.

'Jack Prince is among them,' Crow added quietly.

'That bastard!' Alan Fairfield turned to glare at Crow. His eyes were muddy with a churning anger, and for the first time Crow realized that the Transport Manager had been nursing a real hatred of Jack Prince. He had felt it touch him the first time he had spoken to Fairfield — the angry contempt with which he had spoken of Prince and his 'whore' had given the clue, but now, as Prince was damaging arrangements for which Fairfield was responsible and trespassing on the place where Fairfield held some responsibility, the anger was clear and naked, the hatred exposed. Harris might capitulate; Grainger might under-react; but Crow had the feeling that there was a danger of something else as far as Fairfield was concerned. If anyone could handle the problem it would be this man, accustomed to dealing with roughneck drivers, but equally, if anyone could light a short fuse and cause an explosion, this too could be Alan Fairfield.

'I'll see what I can do,' Crow said. 'I'll contact Plymouth and Exeter and see if we can get more men up here. Meanwhile, try to get hold of Streisman and Foster: I don't think it would be very sensible if they landed here when the demonstration is under way.'

During the next few minutes he used the phone to raise first Plymouth, then the Exeter headquarters. He was forced to report to Grainger that while Plymouth could draft perhaps ten more men to the scene, Exeter personnel were fully committed, and in any case, by the time they reached the site the trouble could well be over. 'My assistant, Inspector Delaval, is on the way here now, but it's unlikely he'll have anyone with him — or at most, maybe two men. I think we'd better proceed on the assumption that we won't be able to prevent them getting on the site. So it's a question of containment only.'

Fairfield came back into the room, his mouth like bent iron. 'I've been on the other phone. Streisman and Foster left just before I called; they'll be here in about eight minutes.'

Crow walked across to the window and peered out over the site. 'Then we'd better move fast.' He pointed towards the sample storage area. 'They're just coming onto the site now. It seems to me they're likely to want as much media coverage as they can get, so let's try to contain things by helping them.'

'*Helping* them?' Fairfield said, in a strangled, frustrated tone.

'Would you rather have a running battle?' Crow snapped. 'Any support staff you have with muscle had better join the ranks with the policemen available. Use the police as the external escort — your own people can move inside that group to offer further protection to Streisman and Foster. Get them across to the helicopter landing-pad as soon as you can.'

Fairfield, his face still mottled with anger, nodded and almost ran from the room. Crow advised Harris and Grainger to see what could be done about barring the reception area, where the food and drink would be available, and then he himself went out to the site, behind Fairfield.

The demonstrators were now grouping into a line, four abreast. They were in no hurry to march across the site, it seemed; the television crew in front of them was incentive enough to give them pause as the crew's director engaged in discussion with Jack Prince and another man. The motives of the media might be wrong, Crow thought grimly, but at least it gave Fairfield time to organize things.

He walked across past the pilot plant and the feed conveyor to the area marked out as a helipad for the occasion: some ruined huts had been cleared, and the concreted section gave a suitable landing-place for the helicopter. Fairfield had worked quickly; he had grouped there some thirty men. They were an ill-assorted group: the police officers in uniform, under the command of an inspector, and some drilling rig operators and drivers, together with suited gentlemen who would obviously be used partly to welcome the visitors and partly to provide a buffer should any ugliness arise on the part of the demonstrators.

Crow introduced himself to the uniformed inspector. 'Don't like this, sir,' the inspector said, rotating his bulk on one heel as he surveyed the scene. 'Too many amateurs, if you know what I mean. Things can flare.'

Crow knew what he meant. The police would raise a small cordon to keep back the demonstrators from the visiting party, and could be trusted to maintain a phlegmatic attitude towards provocation. Civilians were different — and some of the men drafted in by Fairfield looked as though they'd even be happy to take on a group of violent demonstrators.

The police had formed a cordon now, painfully thin, but ringing the landing area. At a given signal, after Streisman's arrival, they would move in protectively; at the same time the inner circle of welcomers and protectors would converge to escort the VIPs. Crow scanned the blue morning sky for the silver gleam of the helicopter, but at the moment there was no sign of it. The demonstrators were starting to move, however; he could hear the chanting begin. It was simple and unimaginative.

'STREISMAN — OUT! STREISMAN — OUT!'

They were marching up the site, two hand-held television cameras moving with them, each raising one clenched fist skywards as they chanted in unison, perhaps seventy or eighty strong, and almost all men.

Perhaps the Bristol Activists wanted and expected a degree of violence.

Crow heard the beat of rotors in the air. He looked up, and saw the helicopter sweeping in over the moorland hills, gleaming silver and red in the sunlight, the blur of the rotors dark against the brightness of the sky as the pilot swung the machine in a long, sweeping curve across the site, hovering briefly at some height, and then tentatively beginning to move away again as the occupants became aware of the snaking group of demonstrators across the site. For a moment Crow thought that common sense was about to prevail, but as the machine still hovered he could imagine the scene inside it. A white-faced Edward Foster would be counselling caution; Myron Streisman, on the other hand, would be stubbornly insistent that he was not going to be turned away by a bunch of long-haired yobbos: *he* hadn't flown thousands of miles to be turned away from his own plant by cranky Reds and worse. The helicopter seemed to waver and swing in the air, and then its nose swung round again and it curved towards the helipad, rotors beating a rhythmic swathe through the mid-morning air. It hovered, swinging slightly, and the sun sent silver and gold reflections of light from its polished sides, flashing across the faces of the waiting men, and dust scurried high, stinging their faces as the helicopter settled noisily, its roar drowning the faded chant of the demonstrators approaching the helipad.

Crow looked around him as the churning airstream slowed under the settling beat of the rotors; hands were raised against eyes, but the men were beginning to move in protectively; behind them the demonstrating group, Jack Prince at its head, was some twenty yards from the policemen, fists raised and punching the air rhythmically, their chant now discernible once more, as the beat of the rotors died.

Under the dome of the helicopter the pilot looked out impassively; Streisman was already opening the door to step out, his rubber-ball body determined, his round face and little eyes hard with displeasure. Foster was behind him, nervousness giving his features a deadening pallidity. They stepped down, and one of the grey-suited men was shaking hands with a curt Myron Streisman, who was gesturing towards the demonstrators and saying something in tones that left no doubt in Crow's mind that he was suggesting that fire-hoses or something similar was the only thing these people understood.

But he and Streisman were being ushered away, and the line of policemen converged inwards, forming a wedge to drive through the demonstrating group, which had now ringed the helipad perimeter, and with Foster and Streisman at the heart of the wedge. Crow hung back, standing near the helicopter as the wedge touched the line of chanting demonstrators and broke it; the challenging fists were still raised, the chanting continued unbroken, but the impassivity of the police cordon was having its effect: the uniforms broke the line, the demonstrators, ugly-faced but not yet moved to violence, moved back.

The wedge marched towards the reception area beyond the laboratories; a frustrated cameraman dragging cable rushed past Crow, but it seemed as though the trouble was going to be minimized as the police cordon drew near the reception area. It was then that a minor scuffle broke out at the back of the cordon; a policeman, his arm being pulled, was dragged back, and one of the drivers on his inside, a heavy-muscled man of twenty-five or so, reached across the beleaguered policemen and threw a punch at a demonstrator. There was a brief struggle, and the antagonists were parted, but the mood was growing uglier among the frustrated demonstrators, and the chanting grew more ragged as obscene epithets were added to the call. Crow skirted the group, hurrying forward towards the building where the reception was to be held. The local bigwigs invited for the junketing would already be inside — they had been arriving for the last twenty minutes or so — but the last thing anyone wanted was a battle outside the reception building. That could lead to the possibility of an invasion of the reception itself — something the television cameramen would be very happy to film, he thought grimly.

The wedge had reached the entrance, Streisman turned and shouted something to the crowd, but Foster was pushing at him, thrusting him inside the building, and with the main objective of their attack vanished the demonstrators began to mill, still chanting, but restless now. Crow forced his way past them, the cordon now flanking the doors opening for him as the police inspector recognized him. 'In you go sir, we made it, should be okay now. Your colleague has already arrived, I understand, sir.'

Delaval. Crow nodded, and brushed past him, casting one glance over his shoulder at the discontented crowd. Fairfield was there, his face twisted with a malignant, taunting triumph, as he glared across the heads at Jack Prince, and Prince was shouting, flailing an arm. Crow closed the door behind him, and the noise was dulled, dying to a confused murmur as he entered the reception room.

They were all there, the local VIPs sipping champagne while an annoyed Myron Streisman mopped his face with a red handkerchief and Edward Foster looked relieved as he sank a glass of sparkling wine. A few of the faces Crow recognized; one man he was surprised to see was Brigadier Leveson but, on reflection, he realized that whether he was an opponent or not Leveson would be invited to this affair because of his position in the county and his involvement, contractually, with the Streisman enterprise.

Crow remained at the back of the room as Myron Streisman made a short speech and the cameras homed in on him; Foster's speech was equally short, and for a politician, to that extent, surprising, but Crow had the impression that the man had been rattled by the demonstration and was now busy making political calculations regarding his involvement with Myron Streisman. He caught sight of Delaval across the room, but could not catch his eye, and then suddenly, as one of the local government councillors was rumbling on about what Streisman could do for the locality, the murmuring outside erupted into a shattering noise as the doors beyond the reception hall crashed open. Crow swung around: he caught a glimpse of two red-faced policemen dragging a man in, frog-marching him away from the reception hall, and into a room leading off on the right. Then two more policemen, with a driver and Alan Fairfield, came bustling in, closing the door behind them to shut out the noise once again, and then standing guard there as Fairfield followed the first entrants into the room to the right.

Crow glanced across; Delaval had seen him. He gestured with his head, and Delaval began to move across. The guests were turning back, the level of chatter now drowning the struggling councillor who was endeavouring to finish his speech, and an empurpled Myron Streisman was glaring across the reception hall towards the doors now guarded by the two policemen.

'Fun and games,' Delaval said in a whisper as he stood behind Crow. 'Did you see who they bustled into that room?'

'Our friend Jack Prince,' Crow said, nodding.

'I think we ought to join them,' Delaval said.

'Two coppers can handle him,' Crow demurred.

'But they can't handle this,' Delaval said, and handed John Crow a small notebook. 'Notes of my conversation with a young lady called Virginia — or Ginny — Morgan.'

* * *

Jack Prince was sitting with his back to the wall beside the desk, against which leaned a burly constable with arms folded impassively across his chest. Prince's black hair seemed damp and matted with sweat, and as he looked up belligerently at Crow, the redness that puffed his cheek just below his left eye was already darkening. His mouth also was swollen, and there was a smear of dried blood on his chin.

Alan Fairfield was standing beside the second policeman, nursing his knuckles with an air of satisfaction. Crow glanced at him, but Fairfield hardly seemed aware of his presence: his eyes were on Prince, and Crow realized that whatever had happened, outside or in this room, it had fed Fairfield's dislike of Prince and slaked his anger to some degree.

Crow introduced himself and Delaval to the two constables and then requested that they leave. They looked doubtful until Crow assured them they'd be staying until it was necessary to call them, and then, taking Fairfield with them, they left the room. Jack Prince glowered at Crow and touched his bruised lip gingerly with his tongue. 'I'm going to bring charges,' he threatened. 'That bastard Fairfield, he started it. There was no need—'

'As far as I could see, your group came hoping for violence,' Crow interrupted. 'Too bad you were the one at the end of it, hey?'

'Fairfield provoked it,' Prince flared, his heavy eyebrows knitting in truculent anger. 'He wanted to have a go at me, and with those coppers beside him he got in among the lads, got hold of me, and hammered me when I was defenceless, unable to get my arms up. The bastard. He'll have to answer to me for this.'

'After you've answered to us,' Crow said softly.

For the first time Prince seemed to realize the men who were speaking to him were connected with matters other than the demonstration at the pilot plant. His glance travelled warily from Crow to Delaval and back again. 'I . . . I got nothing to answer for to you two.'

'We're not so sure of that,' Crow said. 'Inspector—?'

Delaval moved forward. He took the chair out from behind the desk and sat down to face Prince. He removed the notebook from the inside of his jacket and made a great show of consulting it. Then he looked up and gave Jack Prince a friendly grin.

'Quite a girl, Ginny Morgan, isn't she?'

Prince scowled, seemed about to speak, and then thought better of it. Delaval's grin widened, and he said, 'Quite a girl. Anything in trousers, seems to me. Flirted with me, you know — but I was on duty, you see.'

'What the hell's this all about?' Prince demanded, touching his eyelid with a sensitive finger.

'It's just that I've been to see Ginny Morgan again, and asked her a few more questions. Then, as a result of what she said, I asked around a bit more — and I've got some questions to ask you.'

'I got nothing to do with the murder of Fred Norman, so I got no answers to any questions you might ask,' Prince said truculently.

Delaval glanced towards Crow, who nodded. The smile faded on Delaval's mouth and his eyes were an icy blue. 'The questions are pretty simple, my friend. And you'll answer them — or get hauled up to Exeter to answer them.'

Prince's mouth sagged at the corners. 'You're serious!'

'Damned right I am. Let's start with this one: you still stick with your story about being with Ginny the night Fred Norman was killed?'

'It's the truth.'

'She denies it.'

'She's a lying cow. I don't see—'

'She's lying, but you're not. How can you convince me of that?'

A note of crafty triumph suddenly entered Jack Prince's voice. '*I* don't have to prove anything. That bitch is lying; it's up to you to find where the truth lies, not me. I'm telling it to you, but if you don't care to believe the truth when you hear it, that's up to you. Fact is, bloody Ginny Morgan is out of sorts because I haven't been around there since, and she's ready to do me down, and she's nothin' but a little—'

'Hold on, then,' Delaval interrupted, holding up a hand. 'So let's assume I believe your story about being with her that night. What about the night that Freda Park died?'

Prince stared at Delaval, stunned and uncomprehending for several moments. 'Freda . . . ? What the hell has that got to do with . . .'

'I just thought that if you could convince me by telling me the truth about *that* night, I'd be halfway to believing you about the night Norman died.'

Prince cast an appealing glance in Crow's direction, but the impassive stare he received in return made him turn back to Delaval. 'I don't know what the hell you're going on about. I've already told you where I was: in the pub, in the Miner's Arms with Marlene.'

'Hmm.' Delaval consulted his notebook thoughtfully. 'How long were you in the pub that night?'

'Most of the evening.'

'Without a break? I mean, were you in Marlene's company all the time?'

Prince was silent for almost a minute. Then, slowly, he said, 'I wasn't with Marlene all that much that evening. I took her there, but we'd had words, and . . . and I was in the other bar part of the time, playing darts, and I tried to make up with her, but she was niggled and with some other people . . .' He hesitated, thinking. 'And . . . maybe I went out for a stroll by the river a couple of times.'

'By the river?' Delaval asked. 'That isn't what Ginny Morgan says.'

Prince's glance dropped, and he mumbled, 'You don't want to believe what that cow says.'

'So you keep telling me. But do you want to know what she *did* say to me? It was something along these lines. *She* reckons her father was out the night Freda Park was knocked down and killed. Consequently she was expecting someone to visit her. He never turned up, in fact, and she wouldn't tell me his name — but that's how *you* got into the house that night.'

'I never—'

'She says you knocked on the door, she opened it, and you barged in, reaching for her with, I gather from what she says, your usual lack of finesse,' Delaval continued. 'But she had other expectations, and wasn't interested in what you had to offer. There was a bit of a scene, but she managed to turn you out.'

'I was down the pub.'

'Or walking along by the stream?' Delaval's tone was scornful. 'Come off it, Prince. You went up to see that girl, all right. A quarrel with Marlene, anger, heat, and you then thought of Ginny Morgan, always ready for it. You went up there about seven-thirty, man, admit it!'

'All right, damn it, so I went up there! But just because she says it, it doesn't mean she *always* tells the truth! And she's lying about the night Norman was killed! I was with her — and she's just a rotten, conniving, trouble-making little bitch if she says otherwise!'

Delaval smiled; the smile contained no humour. 'Let's say she's naturally perverse. Because she turned you away a *second* time, didn't she?'

Crow could see Prince's male vanity shrinking under Delaval's questions. A man who saw himself as virile and mature being turned away by this girl, not once, but twice in an evening — it was an admission he was unwilling to make. But Delaval persisted, and Crow saw Prince's denials becoming hollower until finally he burst out, 'All right, so I went back! I'd had a few more drinks, and Marlene was still huffy, so I thought if Ginny'd had a bloke up there he'd maybe have finished and she'd let me . . . anyway, I tried the door, but she told me to bugger off, so I went back to the Miner's Arms and—'

'No one recollects seeing you at the pub after nine-thirty,' Delaval said mildly. 'In the street, yes, after the accident, and taking Marlene Park home, but in the pub . . .'

Jack Prince pressed his fingers to his head in a vague irritation. He shook his head. 'All right, I walked back up the town, wandered around a bit, muzzy and niggled as hell, and then I heard the shouting and I came down—'

'And found that Freda had been knocked down and killed?'

Prince nodded. 'I went straight into the pub and got hold of Marlene. She was almost going crazy. And she thought I'd been in the other bar most of the time so I never told her I'd been up after that bloody Ginny—'

'About six weeks before the accident you bought a spray-gun, didn't you?' Delaval asked quietly.

Prince stared at him in surprise. 'How the hell do you know that?'

'Motor accessory shops keep records, and you paid by cheque. And . . . er . . . three days after the accident you bought some paint, I understand.'

Prince shrugged indifferently. 'I've no idea. I might have.'

'Do you have a car, Mr Prince?' Delaval asked.

Jack Prince blinked, then glanced again at Crow. 'What's this about?'

Crow made no reply, and Delaval continued. 'It seems you're accustomed to using Mrs Park's car, but you *do* have one of your own, don't you?'

Prince pulled a disgruntled face. 'Well, I had, but it was a bit of an old banger, and off the road more often than not, so I didn't use it much.'

'So why the spray-gun and the paint?'

'I was doing it up, to sell it.'

'And did you sell it?' When Prince nodded, Delaval said quickly, 'No doubt you can tell us to whom it was sold.'

'Hell, no I can't! What's the big deal? I took it to an auction up at Tavistock and got fifty bloody quid for it! I didn't ask for references, and I didn't ask his name!'

'That really is a pity,' Delaval said quietly.

The room was silent for almost a minute as Jack Prince stared fixedly at Delaval, held by the inspector's ice-blue eyes, transfixed by his own thoughts and the nervous imaginings of what might be going on inside Delaval's head. It was time for John Crow to enter the fray. He walked forward, smiling slightly, diffidently, and there was a deprecating tone in his voice as he said, 'My young colleague here, he has a theory, you see, Mr Prince. It's not one I subscribe to, of course, but I think you need to clear a few points up for him if we're to convince him he's barking up the wrong tree.'

Prince was grateful for Crow's intervention; the warm, soft voice gave him confidence, where Delaval's cold tones had made him edgy, nervous, and caused him to erect defences. 'All right, Superintendent, what do you want to know?'

Crow smiled gently. 'Were you serious when you told me, earlier, that Ginny Morgan and Freda Park were alike in some ways?'

Prince nodded. 'That's right. I told you, Freda was inclined to be influenced by Ginny.'

'Particularly in sexual behaviour . . . though you said, I think, that Freda hadn't . . . misbehaved as Ginny was inclined to do.'

'She used to tease, and flirt . . . usually when she was with Ginny. I told her about it once or twice, when she spoke with men coming out of the pubs — but I wasn't her old man and she told me as much—'

'But you know she didn't die a virgin, surely?' Crow asked. A tremor touched Prince's hands. He looked down at them as though annoyed that they should have betrayed an emotion he wished to hide. 'I don't know anythin' about that.'

'How long have you been living with Mrs Park? Two years, and more? She must have been very distraught after Freda was killed, must have turned to you for comfort and advice — and yet you didn't know that Freda had had sexual intercourse before her death?'

Prince looked up; his eyes were glazed now, as though old horrors were clouding his vision. 'The police came around . . . they spoke to Marlene, and they said . . . but

Marlene was hysterical — she wouldn't believe it, said it was lies, she still saw Freda as just a kid—'

'But you saw her as more than that,' Crow interrupted.

'Of course I did! She was growing, and she knew it and flaunted it, and I told her about it, but she just cheeked me! But I couldn't tell Marlene that, and besides, when I had a go at the coppers in front of Marlene they were forced to admit that the evidence in the report wasn't conclusive—' He fell silent suddenly, flickering quick glances from Crow to Delaval, distrust now staining his glance. 'I don't think I want to talk any more about this. I got a feeling—'

'Which is all my young colleague has, really, a feeling, a theory . . . but perhaps he'll tell us about it now.'

Delaval faced the nervous Prince: his blue eyes were like chips of ice, his mouth grim as he spoke. 'A simple enough theory, Mr Prince. We've been concentrating on Norman, and from a distance we've not been able to judge the space that exists between events, objects, people. Perhaps they were in fact close; closer than we appreciate.'

'I don't know what the hell you're on about.'

'We've seen Freda's death and Norman's death as distant, separated events. But what if they were connected? What if they were bound together? Where would the link be? I think it's you, Mr Prince.'

'You're talking a load of rubbish! Fred Norman—'

'Let's stick with Freda Park for the moment. And let me expound my theory. You'd been living with Marlene Park for two years, and all that time you'd seen this girl ripening to an early womanhood. She was fifteen, yes, but a bonny girl, looking older than her years, and with inclinations that were being aroused by her relationship and friendship with a girl of loose morals — Ginny Morgan. It was inevitable that from time to time you must have looked at Freda in a certain way—'

'That doesn't mean I ever did anything about it,' Prince gasped.

'Let Inspector Delaval unwind his theory, Mr Prince,' Crow said gently, but there was a coldness In his voice that made Prince shiver involuntarily.

'Let's just say you were *aware* of Freda,' Delaval allowed. 'You were really more interested in Ginny Morgan, anyway; whatever your relationship with Marlene Park might be, it didn't inhibit you from desires elsewhere. You lusted for Ginny, and she wasn't particularly resistant — except that one night you went down to the pub with Marlene and quarrelled, moved into the other bar, and decided you'd pay a call on Ginny. You went along there, and she opened the door — but turned you away because she was expecting someone else. And back you went to the pub.' Delaval hesitated, his eyes boring into Prince's. 'Maybe, if you'd been able to get around Marlene then, things might have been all right. But she was still in a mood . . . anyway, half an hour had passed, and you thought maybe Ginny was worth a second try. Or maybe you were angry, wanted to find out who was with her. So you went back up and found that even though Ginny's date hadn't turned up, and she was angry and upset, she still wouldn't have you. She said some pretty wounding, comparative things about you to your face, things that hurt. You left her, mad as hell, your manhood called into question — and then, walking along the street, you met her friend.'

'This is stupid.' Prince licked his dry, swollen lips. 'You can't tie this to me. I—'

'It was dark, sometime after nine,' Delaval continued in a steely voice. 'She was coming along to see Ginny, maybe to suggest she came out with her and walk down to the pub, hanging around outside for her mother and teasing the men as they came out. And you were angry, inflamed, frustrated-yet calm enough and calculating enough to persuade her to go with you, maybe take a ride in your car-which stood, I understand, behind the car park quite often—'

'It wasn't there that night! I'd garaged it up at Selden Hill!'

'So you took her up to Selden Hill, then!' Delaval insisted. 'And in the car you embraced her, started to make love to her. Maybe she encouraged you at first, teased you, as Ginny would have done, as she had seen Ginny do, but then things got a bit out of hand, and you had to use force—'

'It's not bloody well true!' Prince shouted, almost roaring in his panic. 'I never touched the little brat!'

'And then, later, you panicked the way you're panicking now! You took her back, dropped her at home, but she ran down the hill. You knew then you were in trouble. If she reached Marlene, told her what had happened, there'd be your mistress's wrath to face — and also criminal charges of rape of a fifteen-year-old girl. So you panicked, and you drove down the hill and you caught her in the street and you ran her down—'

'It's not true! It's not true! You're trying to frame this—'

The door burst open and Jack Prince almost fell back in his chair. Myron Streisman strode into the room, flanked and followed by a group of hard-faced men. *'You,'* Streisman was saying fiercely, 'if I had my way you'd *hang!'*

* * *

The man was beside himself with rage. They had all clustered in behind him: Brigadier Leveson, Pete Harris, Ray Grainger, Alan Fairfield, the uniformed inspector and a police sergeant, all seemingly swept along by the wake of Myron Streisman's fury. He would have been restraining himself in the reception hall, nerving himself to suffer the speeches and the conversations· and the interviews with newspapers and television, while all the time the mob outside chanted and beat on the doors, but now it was over he had stormed in to confront the man whom they would have described as a ringleader of the demonstration. Only one man had had the sense to hang back out of the way: Edward Foster. A true politician, he was still calculating chances, and he would have known there was little or nothing to be gained by listening to Streisman railing against this man. There were greater political advantages to be obtained by mollifying the other important personages in the reception hall.

Crow was curious as to the reason for Brigadier Leveson's presence. There were two possible explanations — the Brigadier was also a local magistrate, and perhaps felt that his presence in the room was necessary to show how he felt about his public duties; there was also the possibility, however, that his presence on Streisman's coat-tails was dictated by his need perhaps to ingratiate himself and make later negotiations easier, or maybe merely to observe, watch Streisman in action, discover what might needle and upset him. In business, it paid to know your enemy — paid dividends and profits.

He listened to Streisman storming at the man in the chair, a torrent of invective sweeping and lashing over the unfortunate Jack Prince. Crow had stepped to one side, and Delaval too had risen, his eyes on Crow, waiting for a lead, but for the moment Crow was reluctant to pursue the questioning of the demonstration leader.

It was not that he disputed seriously the theoretical reasoning of Delaval; he did not even argue against the theoretical leaps it took, from one assumption to another, for on the basis of facts that they now possessed such leaps were logical, if difficult to prove. It was simply that there was one basic link that was still lacking: they needed that piece of information, that piece of evidence, to support the bridges they had built to span the distances, to measure the relative spaces between Fred Norman and Jack Prince, between Jack Prince and the girl.

A car; a car that had been sold in an auction; a car that might have been sprayed to hide telltale marks of the violence it had done to a girl. There would be no records to cover that respraying, no evidence of that kind. If it had been done by a garage things might have been different . . .

Records . . . relative spaces . . .

Abruptly, John Crow stepped forward, interposing himself between Streisman and Prince. Streisman's face was almost purple, and a line of spittle showed at the corner of his angry, excited mouth. His button eyes glared up into Crow's, not recognizing him in their anger, until Crow silenced him with his words.

'Leading a demonstration — even against Streisman property — is not a hanging matter, Mr Streisman. Not even murder is, these days.'

Streisman stared at him, his mouth working, and then the anger was fading in his eyes, to be replaced by a fog of incomprehension. He scanned Crow's bony, lugubrious features as though he was seeing him for the first time, and as memory came flooding back to submerge still further the passion and anger, so the incomprehension died too. He dabbed nervously at his mouth with the back of his hand. '*Murder?* Superintendent Crow . . . did you say . . . are you questioning this man about Fred Norman's murder?'

The room was still, its atmosphere suddenly electric. Jack Prince twisted in his chair, almost as though he wished to escape, run from the room but was held there by the steel bonds of Myron Streisman's words. Crow smiled thinly. 'We hadn't got around to that before you burst in, but, yes, that's the general idea. We were discussing a theory, you see, which connects this man here—' he gestured towards Jack Prince — 'with the murder of Fred Norman.'

'But I thought . . .' Involuntarily, Myron Streisman glanced back over his shoulder. His eyes settled briefly on Brigadier Leveson, then flickered over his management team, and Crow knew that the American businessman had been weighing in his mind the evidence Crow had already given him, and had been making calculations as to how much it amounted to a motive for murder. Grainger would have come under his consideration, but Crow suspected Streisman would be settling for Pete Harris, the man who had, after all, suppressed the report. He turned back. 'You . . . you think he killed Norman?'

'Well, let's put it like this.' Crow caught Delaval's glance; the detective inspector had frozen, struck with surprise that Crow was about to discuss their theory in front of a group of witnesses, aware that if they were wrong, an action in defamation by Jack Prince would be the least they could look forward to. He was opening his mouth to speak, but Crow's cold glance, warning him, made him bite back the words. 'We have some evidence to support the idea that Prince killed Fred Norman,' Crow said.

'But . . . but what do you base this on?' Streisman asked. 'I mean . . . this man, what connection did he have with Norman?'

'They'd quarrelled in a pub,' Crow said easily. 'But there's more to it than that. You see, we've just been . . . ah . . . discussing another criminal offence that was committed before Fred Norman died. Something that's been assumed to have been a hit-and-run accident.'

Streisman frowned. 'It was one of the sparks for this demonstration . . . You say this man here was involved with that accident?'

'We don't believe it was an accident. Rather, the girl was subjected to, at least, a forcible sexual assault — or rape. And then she was deliberately run down to prevent her speaking and her assailant being brought to account.'

Streisman glared past John Crow to the miserable and panicked Jack Prince, who seemed cowed by the whole proceedings. 'You bastard,' he growled, but Crow was looking past Streisman to one of the faces behind him, and he saw the involuntary movement, the slipping away of a glance, the nervous stepping from one foot to another.

The relative space and distance between people, that was Delaval's point. But what if they were not distant, but closer than most people realized?

'Yes,' Crow continued almost casually, ignoring the alarm in Delaval's eyes, 'the situation was that Freda Park was, in all probability, murdered so that she could not tell her mother, and the police, that she had been raped. I suspect it wasn't a calculated decision to kill her — rather, back in his car, seeing her in the headlights, perhaps, running, sobbing, down the street towards the Miner's Arms he panicked, and the violence in him boiled over in his panic. And then, when Fred Norman got suspicious—'

'But how would Fred get involved?' Streisman asked.

'He'd checked all the garages and come up with nothing — the same way the police had. So we think he checked other records — and realized that the vehicle that killed the girl could have been hidden away for a while, until the killer could do the respray himself. Fred Norman suspected it, and was unwise enough to face the man with his suspicions. That's why Fred Norman was killed. To suppress information that would damage the killer . . .'

Streisman stared at John Crow, suddenly puzzled, aware of the nuances in his tone but unable to fix upon them coherently. He looked past Crow again, to Prince, and then turned around. 'Suppress information . . . ?' His narrow little eyes burned into Pete Harris, and the Exploration Manager flushed, opened his mouth, but in the event said nothing. Streisman turned back to John Crow. 'And this . . . this man killed Fred Norman?'

'Don't you think there was motive enough?' Crow said casually.

Streisman hesitated. 'I suppose . . . if it shows in the records . . .'

'Ah well, that's the problem,' Crow said. 'Records. My colleague, here, he's been checking garages that Norman checked and motor accessory sales and the like, but I think he'd be the first to admit that the evidence he's got is circumstantial — not that circumstantial evidence is any less valuable than direct evidence — but in this case, the evidence isn't, shall we say, conclusive?' He smiled thinly. 'There's still a link missing, a piece of evidence that will support Delaval's theory.'

Pete Harris's voice was husky, and dry. 'What . . . what evidence is that?'

'Well, let's put it in the form of a question. If Fred Norman was killed because he had discovered incriminating evidence relating to the death of Freda Park, what could that evidence be? We know he checked all the garages but so did the police. He wouldn't have checked the sales of motor accessories, as Delaval did: too long and involved a job. But there is one other set of records he would have checked — and probably checked more thoroughly than the police would, because he was more familiar with them and had easier access to them. And, moreover, he would be able to talk to drivers more easily.'

Jack Prince shifted uneasily in his chair and glanced around the room with eyes narrowed in desperation. 'I don't have to stay here to listen to this! I—'

'You're helping us in our enquiries, Mr Prince,' Crow said soothingly. 'Nothing more than that.'

'But you just accused me of murdering two people, and I—'

'No, you misunderstand.' Crow smiled in Delaval's direction. 'The Inspector merely propounded a hypothesis, which, I agree, I found interesting and was prepared to support — except for one thing. The piece of missing evidence. Inspector Delaval has been talking about distances and relative spaces, and establishing the link between you and Freda Park, and you and Fred Norman. But the bridge, the real link is still missing. What made Fred Norman home in on Freda Park's killer?'

Streisman grimaced. 'You're confusing me. I thought you were saying this man here killed Norman — now you're saying . . .'

'What? What am I saying, Mr Streisman?' Crow's tone had become steely. 'I'm saying there's the possibility Freda Park was murdered, and that Norman died because he knew the identity of her killer. But if it *wasn't* Mr Prince here — and in fact we've no clinching evidence to link him with Norman — who was it? Who *did* kill Freda Park? And who could be exposed by Fred Norman, so that he had to kill him too?' Crow glanced around the room at the silent men listening to him. 'I think I can raise my own hypothesis now, not in essence dissimilar from Inspector Delaval's. It goes back to the night Freda Park died, the night Prince visited her friend Ginny Morgan. Ginny was expecting someone else that night, wasn't she, Mr Prince?'

Jack Prince nodded miserably. 'That's why she turned me away.'

'Someone she preferred. Who was it?'

'I don't know. She never told me, but I know someone was seeing her and—'

'You didn't know . . . but had you any suspicion who it might be?' Crow persisted.

Jack Prince looked up; his mouth twisted in an ugly grimace. 'Like you said, I didn't *know,* but I had my suspicions—'

'And did *he* know about *you?'*

Someone shifted behind Crow, a nervous, involuntary shuffle. Prince's eyes flickered past the policeman, searching. 'I don't know. He could have done . . . or maybe with him it was just suspicion, too. She's a close bitch, that Ginny Morgan.'

'Well, let me put another hypothesis to you, Mr Prince, about that night. Much the same as Inspector Delaval suggests but slightly different. You went up to Ginny's and she was expecting someone else. I wonder what would have happened if you had been in her house when he arrived?'

Prince glared at him. 'I don't understand.'

Crow shrugged. 'If you got there just before him, and he arrived, seeing you go in, what might he have thought?'

Comprehension dawned in Prince's eyes. 'He might have thought she was entertaining me instead of him!'

'Would that have made him angry?'

Prince grinned wolfishly. 'It would've made *me* mad as hell! Why not him?'

Crow nodded. 'Ginny Morgan says he didn't ever turn up that night — he wasn't there when you returned later, was he? So let's take Inspector Delaval's assumptions and change them slightly. This man goes to Ginny's, sees you enter, assumes he is out in the cold, and angrily, turns to leave. But who should be coming along the road, but Ginny's friend, Freda! *If* this man knows local people, and if he knows Ginny well, it's more than likely he'll have at least *met* Freda. She is accustomed to teasing men the way Ginny does, though without following through. So she flirts with this man, goes in his car with him — it's probably parked somewhere away from Ginny's place to avoid gossip — and then, by the time she finds herself in trouble, is unable to do anything about it. He rapes her. He drives her back to the village and sets her down. Only then does he realize the trouble he's in if she talks and her distress, as she runs towards the Miner's Arms, makes him realize she *will* talk. So he runs her down.'

There was a short silence. Delaval had been watching Crow closely. Now he spoke. 'If we go back to relative spaces and distances again, what you're saying is, there might have been someone else, closer than we've perceived, to Freda, and Prince—'

'And Fred Norman,' Crow said, nodding. 'Someone who has certain . . . er . . . qualifications we can look for. First, if he isn't a local man, he must be someone who knows Ottershaw and its inhabitants fairly well, and uses the local pub. He must have thus had the opportunity of knowing Ginny Morgan and *meeting* Freda Park, at the very least, because it's unlikely she would have gone off with a total stranger. Secondly, he must be a man able to repair his car himself — or have it repaired, perhaps-to cover the damage that would probably have been occasioned by the running down of Freda Park. Thirdly, he must be someone with whom Norman was in contact, and whose records Norman must have inspected, and fourthly . . . he is probably a man with little liking for his rival, Jack Prince. If we can point to someone with these qualifications . . .'

The chair went over with a crash as Jack Prince stood up. His eyes were bulging, a flush of anger had stained his face and he raised his hands, fingers clenched, trembling violently. He was glaring past Crow, and his mouth was working silently as the obscenities built up in his head. Then he flung himself forward, past Crow, to crash into Myron Streisman.

The American businessman staggered sideways, off balance, throwing up his hands to ward off the expected attack, and at his side Brigadier Leveson lurched forward in an attempt to restrain Jack Prince. But the man was already shouldering his way past, pushing Pete Harris aside in his violent attempt to reach the man he wanted.

'You bastard!' He shouted in a high, raging tone. 'You killed them both, and you would've set me up for it!'

Alan Fairfield met his attack with all the simmering hate and fear that must have been affecting him for months. As Prince surged in at him he swung violently with his right hand, catching Prince on the shoulder, and then followed up with a series of blows that would normally have deterred an attacker, but Prince was beside himself with rage. The fears that had been aroused in him by the questioning of Crow and Delaval now burst forth in a crashing anger that demanded he beat Alan Fairfield into submission to assuage his fury, and both men were locked together, their faces inches apart, contorted, strained, shouting. Then they fell, writhing obscenely together on the ground, fists beating at heads and throats and bodies, until the policemen in uniform dragged them apart and they were forced from the room, to leave a shaken, white-faced Myron Streisman, half-supported by Brigadier Leveson, turning for an explanation to Detective Superintendent Crow.

* * *

It was another week before he was able to give the American businessman a full explanation. He and Delaval had then had time to question Fairfield further, to inspect the company vehicle records, check with the drivers in the manner that Fred Norman had done, and reveal the discrepancy in mileage records and usage from the drivers' log-books. The vehicle in question was a Land-Rover; Fairfield had resprayed it himself and amended the records kept in his office to show that the Land-Rover had been off the road on the relevant date. In his check, instigated after his argument with Prince in the Miner's Arms, Norman had discovered the discrepancy and eventually confronted Fairfield with it, asking for an explanation. The Transport Manager had already killed once, and now, to keep that secret, he killed Fred Norman at Norman's cottage and disposed of his body in the tailings pond. Ginny Morgan had confessed to Delaval that her other lover was Alan Fairfield, and confirmed that Freda Park had met him occasionally and, indeed, had said she 'fancied' him. And the case against Fairfield would proceed along the lines outlined by Crow to the gathering at the pilot plant.

'We could do with more men like Norman,' Streisman said moodily. 'A real company man.'

'He was certainly busy those last months,' Crow agreed. 'Negotiating with Leveson and Prince and the others, preparing a report on Craydon Engineering, and at the same time working over those garage records until he found the answer to the killing of Freda Park. But he was hardly making himself popular, was he?'

'Business has got nothing to do with popularity,' Myron Streisman said harshly. 'But efficiency and honesty that's another matter. Pete Harris is out, and I'll never employ him again: he put his own personal future before the company good. He's finished. And so is Grainger — at best incompetent, at worst, criminal, in the way he handled the Craydon Engineering contribution.'

'And the Brigadier?' Crow asked softly.

Myron Streisman squinted thoughtfully through the windows of his Exeter office. 'The Brigadier isn't as bad as he's been painted. He can cause us trouble . . . but it looks as though maybe we can work something out, maybe bring his interests closer to ours. The important thing is to get the project finished . to both our benefits. We'll see eye to eye, I think . . .'

'And Mr Foster?'

Streisman walked nervously around the room. He shrugged. 'He might have made a mistake, recommending

Craydon to us. But . . . he's got political weight and we still need him.'

'So honest dealing is a matter of degree?' Crow asked cynically.

'No,' Myron Streisman denied with a shake of his head. 'It's just that business is business.'

And that, Crow explained to Delaval, largely left Jack Prince and Marlene Park out in the cold. Their relationship was now doomed anyway, and the success of their campaign was likely to be dissipated in bickering, and certain charges brought as a result of the violence at the Ottershaw plant. But at least Crow and Delaval had done what Myron Streisman had asked: point to the problems in his company, and bring to book the murderer of Fred Norman by the time the plant opened.

'Though I was wrong with my theory,' Delaval said. 'I pointed to the wrong man.'

'But the right theory,' Crow insisted. 'So only a little distance from the truth.'

Delaval grinned. 'And distance—?'

'Is only relative.'

THE END

INSPECTOR JOHN CROW SERIES

Book 1: A LOVER TOO MANY
Book 2: ERROR OF JUDGMENT
Book 3: THE WOODS MURDER
Book 4: MURDER FOR MONEY
Book 5: MURDER IN THE MINE
Book 6: A COTSWOLDS MURDER
Book 7: A FOX HUNTING MURDER
Book 8: A DARTMOOR MURDER

More Inspector John Crow books coming soon!
Join our mailing list to be the first to hear about them
http://www.joffebooks.com/contact/

Thank you for reading this book. If you enjoyed it please leave feedback on Amazon, and if there is anything we missed or you have a question about then please get in touch. The author and publishing team appreciate your feedback and time reading this book.

Our email is office@joffebooks.com

http://joffebooks.com

Follow us on Facebook www.facebook.com/joffebooks

We hate typos too but sometimes they slip through.
Please send any errors you find to
corrections@joffebooks.com
We'll get them fixed ASAP. We're very grateful to eagle-eyed readers who take the time to contact us.